J. B. Calchman lives and works in London.

J.B. CALCHMAN

Vampire Heart

PUFFIN BOOKS

PUFFIN BOOKS

Published by the Penguin Group
Penguin Books Ltd, 27 Wrights Lane, London W8 5TZ, England
Penguin Putnam Inc., 375 Hudson Street, New York, New York 10014, USA
Penguin Books Australia Ltd, Ringwood, Victoria, Australia
Penguin Books Canada Ltd, 10 Alcorn Avenue, Toronto, Ontario, Canada M4V 3B2
Penguin Books (NZ) Ltd, Private Bag 102902, NSMC, Auckland, New Zealand

On the World Wide Web at: www.penguin.com

Penguin Books Ltd, Registered Offices: Harmondsworth, Middlesex, England

Kiss of the Vampire first published by Puffin Books, 1996
Dance with the Vampire first published by Puffin Books, 1996
Touched by the Vampire first published by Puffin Books, 1999
Kiss of the Vampire, Dance with the Vampire, Touched by the Vampire
first published in one volume, 1999
1 3 5 7 9 10 8 6 4 2

'It Is Something to Have Wept' by G. K. Chesterton, copyright © G. K. Chesterton,
reprinted by permission of A. P. Watt Ltd on behalf of the Royal Literary Fund.

Set in Sabon

Made and printed in England by Clays Ltd, St Ives plc

British Library Cataloguing in Publication Data
A CIP catalogue record for this book is available from the British Library

ISBN 0–140–38627–0

CONTENTS

IT IS SOMETHING
TO HAVE WEPT

by G. K. Chesterton

It is something to have wept as we have wept,
and something to have done as we have done;
it is something to have watched when all have slept,
and seen the stars which never see the sun.

It is something to have smelt the mystic rose,
although it break and leave the thorny rods;
it is something to have hungered once as those
must hunger who have ate the bread of gods:

To have known the things that from the weak are furled,
the fearful ancient passions, strange and high;
it is something to be wiser than the world,
and something to be older than the sky.

Lo, and blessed are our ears for they have heard:
yea, blessed are our eyes for they have seen:
let the thunder break on human, beast and bird,
and lightning. It is something to have been.

beautifull

Kiss of the
Vampire

For Carla and Andrew

THE FUNERAL

OAKPORT, MAINE

THE CHURCHYARD WAS perched on the top of a cliff. A line of black spruce trees was all that prevented it from slipping into the ocean. Down below, the water swirled and a mist rose, like steam, seeping into the crags of the dark rock as it made its ascent.

Three fresh gravestones had been set into the earth that morning, and now, in the last of the light, four figures approached them. The preacher led the way, his robes skimming the damp ground as he took his position. The others followed: a woman whose ill-assorted clothes might have come from a dressing-up box; a tall man whose thick, blond hair was like a flame against his dark coat; and last, a child, a boy, struggling to keep up, tumbling forward towards the graves.

There was another person in that churchyard, hidden among the spruces at the cliff-edge. His eyes strained to watch the funeral procession. The preacher had begun to speak, but there was no hope of hearing him from this distance. The old man's crumpled mouth opened and closed, fish-like, his words seemingly making no dent in the air. The others huddled together, as if gaining strength from each other. The watcher had an overwhelming desire to turn and run, but he knew that it was out of the question. Whatever he felt, the child was more important.

A sudden shot of pain bore through him and he lurched back, falling on to the bed of pine needles. It was the same sensation as before – as if his veins were overloaded with blood. He froze, numb, as the pain took hold. His eyes locked on the circling branches above. He let the scent of the pines wash into him. Gradually, the tenseness subsided and the pain crept away.

Relieved, he clawed back up to his feet, his hand brushing the bandage on his neck. As he steadied himself, he drew his hand away and saw that the tips of his fingers were scarlet.

When his eyes returned to the funeral party, he saw the preacher beckon the man to the graves. In response, the man stooped to the ground and grabbed a handful of earth from the mound beside the first grave. He stepped to the edge of the hole and released the earth. The watcher imagined the echo as it thudded against the coffin below.

The man repeated his actions at the next grave. The rain had started again but, unflinch-ing, the preacher, woman and child stood and watched. The man moved on to the third grave.

This time as he threw the earth, it would not move from his hand. He tried again, but still it would not shift. He turned and the watcher could see the look of horror on his face.

The woman rushed forward, leaving the boy's side. She seized the man by the wrist and tugged at the earth. Suddenly, it came away, leaving a dark stain. The woman twisted the man's palm up towards the sky and, as the rain fell, scrubbed away as if she were washing a child's fingers.

The boy stood alone in the centre of the churchyard, trembling. Instinctively, the watcher moved to the edge of the trees. Could this be the chance he had been waiting for? He quickly calculated the distance between them. He could do it. It would all be over then. The circle would be complete.

But if he failed? If he was seen? The others might be scared, but that wouldn't stop them. It would all begin again. And the child would be lost to him for ever. He recoiled, with a pain far worse than that from the blood-wound. He could not do this. Not yet. He would have to make new plans.

The preacher was leading them back into the church. The woman turned and took the child's left hand. The man followed behind. As the rain grew heavier, they started to run. Once again, the boy struggled to keep pace. As the heavy church door slammed shut behind them, a bolt of lightning sliced through the sky. Thunder followed.

Alone in the churchyard, the watcher stepped out from his hiding-place. Lumps of earth clung to his boots. He realized how foolish he had been to think he could have captured the boy. He could move only slowly now, as once he had through the ocean, the undertow tugging at his legs. The thunder and lightning crashed around him as he stood before the three graves. The others' footprints had already been washed away.

He watched the water worming its way into the newly carved marble and shuddered as he read the inscriptions.

Adam Culler, 1952–1995. Beloved husband of Charlotte and father of Alexander and Charles . . .

Charlotte Baines Culler, 1954–1995 . . .

Alexander Culler, 1978–1995. Son of Adam and Charlotte. 'In their death they were not divided' . . .

The tears that had begun to form froze with the shock of reading his own name. His finger traced the carved letters on the icy marble. *Alexander Culler.* He still could not believe what had happened.

As another flash of lightning struck, the pain within him seemed to respond, pushing through his veins and towards the wound. And the warm river of blood gushed from his neck to his shoulder and down to join the sea of mud below.

CHAPTER I

ST DOVE'S, CORNWALL
SEVERAL WEEKS LATER

'YOU DON'T KNOW anything about him.'
'And if I don't ask, I never will!'
'You can't.'
'I can.'
'He could be dangerous.'
'Don't be daft.'
'Remember what happened to Juliet.'
'Yes, but . . .'
'But you don't believe in . . .'
The argument, if it could be called that, was interrupted by the door opening. Just another couple of tourists coming into the Green Room to get a coffee and something to eat after a stroll along the beach. As Greeny settled them with a menu and began to chit-chat, Ella remained by the window, watching the boy outside.

For the past week, they had argued about him. Ella was curious to know his story, but Greeny believed he was best left alone. Of course, her aunt had strong views about boys and men, after the latest upheavals in her own personal life. But

Ella wasn't just being awkward or stubborn. There was something about the boy which drew her to watch him, even though he never appeared to notice her.

The steam from the coffee machine had clouded up the window and Ella wiped her hand over the pane to make a peep-hole. He was standing in the usual place, his eyes locked on the ocean. There were plenty of people who came down to look at the sea, but this was different. He seemed mesmerized by the waves.

It was a blustery morning and the wind twisted the long dark strands of his hair. Otherwise, he was as still as a statue, his hands buried deep in the pockets of his coat. His clothes were another mystery. In spite of the breeze, it was a warm summer's day. Everyone else was wandering around in T-shirts and shorts, but he wore a thick winter coat and heavy black boots. Both were scuffed with dirt much darker than the sand.

'Ella.'

Ella turned and could tell from Greeny's expression that she had been trying to attract her attention for a while. She followed the line of Greeny's gaze and went over to pick up the two coffee cups and take them over to the couple. She placed them on the table, smiling vacantly, and returned to the window. It had steamed up again and again she made herself a porthole.

It was infuriating the way his hair flapped

around his face, preventing her from gaining a proper view of it. She knew from other times how handsome he was. Perhaps it was the unnatural stillness, but he seemed to her like a sculpture, his features soft and smooth as aged stone.

'Excuse me. Excuse me, miss . . .'

Ella turned, unable to blot out the anger from her expression. Why couldn't they leave her alone?

'We're ready to order now. Can you tell your mother, we'd like . . .'

Deciding it wasn't worth correcting them, Ella noted their requests and relayed them to Greeny, who was washing pots in the kitchen. She didn't stay long, anxious to resume her look-out. As she regained her position at the window, she saw with sadness that the boy had gone. She looked down the beach and noticed that the tide had turned. He always left just as the tide started to come in.

The door to the café swung open and three boys ambled inside. They had been surfing and were still wearing their wet suits, rolled down to their waists, along with bright T-shirts and 'bajas' – thick, brightly striped, hooded shirts.

'How was the surf?' the male tourist inquired, looking up from his soup.

'Spectacular,' one of the boys answered, running his hands through his curly blond hair and making his way over to Ella. 'Hello, stranger,' he said, taking her in his arms and nuzzling her neck.

'Ooh, that explains it!' giggled the woman. 'She's been staring out of that window like a zombie. I thought something was wrong, but she was obviously watching you!'

Everyone laughed but Ella.

'Did you see me out there? What did you think?'

Ella unwrapped his arms from her waist. 'You were great, Teddy. I'll go get some Cokes.'

'So, have you heard about the Vampire of St Dove's?' Ella heard Teddy ask the couple, as she opened up the refrigerator.

'I was reading about that in our guidebook,' the man replied. 'It was during plague times, wasn't it? He roamed the streets of the town, drinking the blood of the dying.'

His wife tutted. She clearly didn't think this was a suitable mealtime conversation.

'Oh yes, everyone knows about that old vampire,' breezed Teddy. 'I'm talking about the new vampire!'

The man looked up in curiosity. Greeny shot a warning look at Teddy, but he was on a roll.

'Oh yes, indeed! It happened a little over a week ago. A girl walking home late at night . . . you get the picture? Next morning, she was found by the side of the road, with two little puncture marks in her neck.'

The man gasped and the woman went pale.

'She was alive,' Greeny interrupted.

'Barely,' Teddy retorted, 'and she hasn't spoken since.'

Ella was about to pass Teddy a Coke when he wandered over to the table and rested a hand on the woman's shoulder. 'Want to know the best bit? The girl was a waitress here.'

The woman turned a shade of green, pushed back her chair and rushed out into the air. The man followed, frowning. Greeny ran to the door and looked on helplessly as the couple headed away along the beach.

'Teddy Stone, you're bad for business,' Greeny said, closing the door.

Teddy laughed and drained his Coke. 'Please, Mrs Green, can Ella come out to play?' he said, affecting a child's voice.

Greeny began to smile. 'Off you go, then,' she said.

The boys ambled back out on to the beach, where the sun was shining brightly. Ella followed, her hand in Teddy's.

'You have a good time,' laughed Greeny, going off to clear the debris of the tourist couple's lunch.

Ella said nothing. She couldn't get him out of her head – the mysterious boy who came each day to watch the sea.

CHAPTER II

ELLA LAY BACK on the rug, her dark sunglasses filtering the strong afternoon sunlight, and tossed the paperback to one side. She must have read the same sentence a hundred times. She couldn't concentrate at all. The heat seemed to have sapped all her energy.

She reached into her bag and fumbled for her Walkman. It was already loaded with a tape she'd put together of all her favourite songs. She slipped in the ear plugs, closed her eyes and turned up the volume, luxuriating in the familiar music.

She hadn't been listening for long when she became aware of a shadow over her, blocking the sun. She opened her eyes and removed the earphones.

'Ashley. How was the water?'

'Perfect!' Ashley Stone beamed, patting herself dry. 'I just love the water. Not quite like the boys, of course. They're obsessed! But it's so refreshing. Oh, Ella . . . I'm sorry. I forgot you can't swim.'

'That's all right.'

'I never imagined Teddy would go out with somone who didn't like the water,' Ashley said, combing her hair. 'Of course, he'd love to teach you.'

Ella had no desire for Teddy to teach her to swim. Still, there was no point in arguing with Ashley. She would soon latch on to a new topic of conversation.

'Scott's going to teach me how to surf,' Ashley continued, opening a tube of sun cream and massaging it over her shoulders. 'Now, that should be fun! I mean, Daddy tried to teach me when Teddy and I were both little. And Teddy's even given me one or two lessons. But there's more of an incentive for Scott to show me . . . if you know what I mean!'

Realizing that there was going to be no end to Ashley's chatter, Ella decided to make herself comfortable and rolled over, sprawling on the rug.

'Shall I do your back?' Ashley inquired.

Ella nodded. Ashley squirted a cold blob of sun screen on to her warm shoulders.

'You've become so quiet lately, Ella,' gabbled Ashley, drawing the cream down Ella's shoulder-blades. 'Is it this vampire business? You know, I'm sure there's a logical explanation. I mean, I know all about the stories of St Dove's during the plague, but I'm sure that's all they were . . . stories. And now! Don't get me wrong, I'm scared too. I mean perhaps there is some maniac on the loose. Unless –'

'Let's not talk about it,' Ella said. 'Why don't

you tell me what you're going to wear to the party at Smugglers' Cove?'

'The grand opening of the Cave, you mean? Well, let me see . . .'

Ella had struck gold. There was nothing Ashley enjoyed discussing more than clothes. As she rambled on, weighing up the pros and cons of one outfit against another, Ella closed her eyes and let the words drift over her.

She was brought to attention by a shower of icy drops on her body. She twisted round as Teddy leaned over her. He had just come out of the sea and was dripping wet. She was about to protest but he silenced her with a kiss. Over his shoulder, she saw Ashley rubbing cream into Scott's shoulders. Things were getting pretty serious between the two of them.

Jeff, meanwhile, was encountering some difficulty, rubbing sun cream into the well of his back. He had broken up with his latest girl-friend, Laura, the previous week and was taking it hard. Feeling sorry for him, Ella offered to help. He ran over gratefully and crouched down in front of her, eager to chat. Sighing, Teddy sauntered off to fetch a drink from the cool box.

'So, what's going on tonight?' Scott asked Teddy as he passed.

'I thought we might drive down the coast. Apparently, there's this great new place on the Lizard. There's a barbecue and a live band tonight.'

There were nods and sounds of enthusiasm from everyone but Ella. 'I have to work tonight,' she said and then, in response to Teddy's groans, 'you knew that.'

Of course he acted dumb, making it seem as though she was spoiling everyone's fun.

'Look, you can go without me,' Ella said, grabbing a Coke.

'I didn't start going out with you so that I could spend my evenings alone,' Teddy snapped. As if on cue, the others turned away and began their own conversations.

'Look, Teddy,' Ella said calmly, 'things are hard for Greeny right now. We don't know how long Juliet will be away and, in case you hadn't noticed, the café is busier than ever. People come from miles around to see where "the vampire" claimed his first victim. It's morbid but it is good for business. Just try to be patient, Teddy.'

'Yeah, I suppose,' he said, looking deep into her eyes. 'It's just difficult to be patient where you're concerned. You know I want to be with you all the time.'

'Except when you're surfing,' Ella said, trying to lighten the mood.

'Don't joke,' Teddy replied. 'I've never felt this way about anyone before.' He drew her face up towards his and they kissed.

'Why don't you guys head out to that place at the Lizard tonight and if I can get away later, I will,' Ella offered.

The others agreed and decided it was time they were heading home to get ready. They packed up their stuff and started up the cliff path to where Scott's red MG and Teddy's black VW convertible were parked.

In a moment, the stereos were clicked into action, the shades were in place and the two cars were racing back to the other side of town. With some of Teddy's favourite rock music blaring from the stereo, it was too noisy to speak and Ella lost herself in her own thoughts. Before she knew it, Teddy was bringing the VW to a halt at the back of the Green Room.

'Wow, is that a Harley?' he said, flipping up his sun-glasses and ogling the motor bike, propped to one side of the café door.

Teddy jumped out of his seat and went over to have a closer look. The bike was somewhat battered and rusted, but it retained its classic style. 'This baby hasn't seen the light of day for a while,' he decided. 'I wonder who it belongs to.'

'Who cares?' snorted Ashley, from the back of the car. 'You'd never catch me riding on that heap of junk. It looks like it's going to fall to pieces any moment.'

'You just don't understand, sis,' Teddy said, smiling. He turned to Ella. 'I'll phone you when I get in with the details of this place. You'll see if you can come along later?'

She nodded and kissed him goodbye. He

climbed back into the car and started it up, honking the horn loudly as he drove away. Ella pushed open the door to the café and stepped inside, her eyes taking a moment to grow accustomed to the darkness. The café was empty, but Ella knew from experience that it wouldn't be for much longer. In an hour the place would be full of kids from all over town. She was about to step into the kitchen when Greeny came out of it. Seeing Ella, she smiled broadly.

'Did you have a nice afternoon?'

Ella nodded. 'I know I'm a bit late. I'll just go up to the flat and grab a shower and I'll be ready to help.'

'It's OK, love,' Greeny said, 'I've got some good news. I've hired someone new! And, better yet, they can start tonight.'

'Oh, that's great!' Ella said. 'Who is she?'

'Come and see,' Greeny said, pushing open the kitchen door.

Ella followed her inside and was amused to see that Greeny's new helper was already elbows deep in washing-up – a shock of dark hair bowed over the sink.

'Alex,' Greeny said, 'I'd like you to meet my niece. Ella, this is Alex Culler.'

Ella smiled as Alex turned. Then her heart missed a beat. It wasn't a girl at all but a boy; the boy she had been watching each day. She had imagined their meeting a hundred times, but not here, not like this. She didn't know what to say. Just looking at him made her uneasy.

'I'll go and . . . change the coffee filters,' Greeny said, winking at Ella before the kitchen door swung shut behind her.

Ella felt trapped. This was what she had wanted – a chance to be alone with him, to ask him who he was and where he had come from and why he watched the sea as if his life depended upon it. And yet, she couldn't bring herself to speak, let alone ask such probing questions.

'She told me, you know.'

'What?'

Ella couldn't decide whether she was more surprised because he had struck up a conversation, or because he had an American accent.

'Greeny. She told me what happened to Juliet.'

Ella was silent. If only she could think of something, *anything*, to say.

'I'm sorry,' he said. 'Would you rather not talk about it?'

'No! No, it's OK.'

Now he seemed unable to find the right words.

'Do you . . .' she began, 'do you believe in . . .'

Catching his eye, she was unable to finish the sentence. He was looking at her with such an intensity, as if he was staring deep into her, through her.

'Do I believe?' He repeated the question to himself and paused before answering. 'I guess I don't know what I believe any more.'

She waited for him to continue, to explain what he meant. But he turned away and busied himself with the things in the sink. Ella had the feeling that once again she was watching him from the other side of the window and he was completely unaware of her existence.

LATER THAT NIGHT ...

I HAVE SENSED the hunger building all day and, as night falls, I know what is going to happen. When the town is dark and almost deserted, I make my way to the cliff edge. There's a place I've found there where I can sit and listen to the waves. The sound scares me, yet it draws me to it.

I lose track of the time I spend there, lulled by the noise of the sea and the patterns of the shifting darkness, broken only by the flashes from the lighthouse. At times like this, I can't help but think of the journey I have made. Such a long way. When I think of who I was, of where I've come from, I marvel at the strange paths my life has taken.

Life. It's hard to believe that this is life and not death. And yet, there have been better times. Perhaps there can be again.

The hunger is building. It's like this every time. It starts small, like an itch, a dull ache, inside me. Gradually, it becomes more acute. Finally, it tears through me, pulsating with a life of its own. Then, I have only one need and there is only one way of satisfying it.

I see beyond the cliff-top trees. I see deep

down into the sea. I see to the end of this road. And I see the girl, walking towards me through the shadows. I see the girl and I know that my hunger will soon be satisfied.

I decide to wait, to let her come to me. The trees will give us shelter, away from the road. I *can* wait. Now that I know she is coming.

She draws level with me and I reach out, taking her hand. She turns. For an instant we stand face to face. We are mirror images of each other – the same height, the same long dark hair. I smile. I want to win her trust.

It is over quickly for her. Time runs differently for me. I am over-anxious and her silky hair slips through my fingers when I try to lift it away from her neck. I try again and, this time, succeed. I have no need to restrain her now. She is perfectly still. It is as if she knows everything.

My lips brush her neck and I can feel the flow of blood beneath the skin. I bite. She jerks at the impact but does not move again. Quickly, I draw the blood up towards my lips. I drink thirstily.

I know when to stop. I step back and see that she has closed her eyes. The breeze lifts the threads of hair from her neck and I watch this, entranced, for a time.

Then I lay her down where I know they will find her.

CHAPTER III

'I CAN'T BELIEVE you hired him,' Ella said as she and Greeny sat down to breakfast the following morning.

'No, but you're glad I did, aren't you?' her aunt replied, sipping coffee from her favourite pottery mug.

Ella blushed. 'Yesterday, you were telling me how dangerous he was. What made you change your mind?'

'Yes, that was wrong of me. I shouldn't have judged him on his appearance. I really ought to know better than that by now. He came in here and asked about the vacancy – he'd seen the card in the window – and he was just very sweet.'

Ella smiled, thinking back to the previous evening. In the time she had spent with Alex, they had scarcely spoken. He had told her next to nothing about himself. And yet, she felt more strongly than ever that there was something special about him, something which connected the two of them.

'You like him!' Greeny said, pouring another mug of coffee and offering Ella a freshly baked muffin.

'What's not to like?' Ella said, blushing.

'And where does this leave Mr Stone?' her aunt inquired.

Ella shrugged. 'When I started going out with Teddy, it was like the most magical thing, a fairy-tale. I mean, everyone wants to be with him, but *he* chose *me*. And he is very handsome and everything . . .'

'But . . .' persisted Greeny.

'But I'm not exactly sure why we're together any more.'

Ella and Teddy had been going out with each other for almost a year. Lately, however, the spark seemed to have died. They still had fun, but the old excitement wasn't there. Perhaps that was what intrigued her about Alex. Getting to know him would be like starting to unravel a complex mystery; whereas she could predict pretty well all of Teddy's thoughts and actions and moods.

'Well, just be careful,' was Greeny's advice. 'Teddy Stone won't take rejection easily and we still don't know very much about Alex.'

'You're not going to tell me again that he's dangerous, are you?'

'No, but he is hurting. I can feel it. And he's run away from something, something bad. You'd better tread carefully, for his sake . . . and your own.'

Greeny buried herself in her newspaper and Ella looked out through the window to the beach. The sun had already cast a pool of gold over the sand. It had all the makings of a perfect day.

They cleared up the breakfast things and were just setting out the menus when Alex drew up outside on his bike. He came inside, unstrapping his helmet.

'You're bright and early,' Greeny said. 'Coffee?'

'No thanks,' Alex said, walking past them into the kitchen. He didn't even say hello to Ella. She felt her spirits sink.

Greeny placed a comforting hand on Ella's shoulder. 'Rome wasn't built in a day, love,' she whispered.

They burst into giggles. The giggles grew into laughter until Ella could feel her sides aching.

'What are you two laughing about?' Teddy asked, closing the door of the café behind him. He kissed Ella and grabbed a chair. Greeny said she'd get him some coffee and disappeared, still chuckling, into the kitchen.

'Where did you get to last night?' Teddy inquired after Greeny had gone.

'I'm sorry,' Ella said, feeling the hysteria subside. 'I couldn't get away. We had a really busy night. Did you have a good time?'

'Without you?' Teddy shrugged. 'Impossible! I see the Harley's still outside . . .'

Greeny reappeared from the kitchen with a mug of coffee for Teddy. She beckoned Alex to follow her.

'Teddy,' Greeny said, 'I'd like you to meet Alex Culler. He's going to be helping out around here. Alex, this is . . . one of our regulars, Teddy Stone.'

The boys shook hands. Ella suddenly felt awkward. Until yesterday, Alex had been her secret. And secrets were few and far between in a town as small as St Dove's. Now that Alex was working at the café, everything was going to change.

'Culler,' Teddy said. 'You're related to the old guy who repairs clocks in the high street?'

Alex nodded but said nothing. Ella smiled. Why should Teddy be any more successful than her in getting Alex to talk about himself?

'Is that your Harley outside?' Teddy persisted.

'Not exactly,' Alex said.

'It belongs to Gabriel Culler,' Greeny explained, seeing that Alex's reticence was starting to infuriate Teddy. 'It was rusting to pieces in his garage. Alex cleaned it up and it seems to be going OK.'

'Maybe I could borrow it sometime,' Teddy said.

'Maybe.'

'Here's an idea,' Teddy said. 'Have you heard of Smugglers' Cove? It's a theme park – the closest thing in England to Disneyworld. My family owns it and we're having a little party there on Saturday night to celebrate the opening of our new night-club. Why don't you come along, Alex? It'll be a good chance to get to know everyone. Ella will fill you in on all the details.'

'OK,' Alex said, retreating into the kitchen.

'Talkative guy!' Teddy exclaimed as the door swung shut after Alex. 'What's his story?'

'Maybe he doesn't have a story,' Ella said, doing her best to act uninterested.

'Everyone has a story! And I'd say Alex Culler has a very interesting story indeed. How do you suppose he's related to the old man – what's his name, Gabriel? – for a start?'

Before Ella could come up with an answer, the door burst open and a young boy, perhaps eight or nine years old, ran into the café. He was out of breath and his eyes were bulging. He tried to speak but he couldn't get the words out.

Greeny poured him a glass of water. 'Here, sit down, tell us what's wrong.'

The boy shook his head. Without speaking, he ran over and grabbed Teddy's arm, indicating for him to follow.

'Careful!' Teddy said. 'This shirt cost a fortune.'

He followed the boy out on to the beach. Ella and Greeny rushed to the door of the café. Alex came out to see what was going on and joined the others at the doorway, watching as Teddy ran after the boy up the cliff path. They disappeared for some minutes. When they reappeared, Teddy was carrying a girl's body slumped over his shoulders.

'It's Lucy Vale,' Teddy gasped. 'She's unconscious, maybe . . .'

'Oh my . . .' Greeny interrupted, 'I'll call an ambulance.'

Alex rushed over to help Teddy, while Ella tried to soothe the young boy. He was still in a state of shock.

'Here, put her down over here,' Greeny instructed, tapping the buttons on the phone. 'Yes, I need an ambulance . . . The Green Room Café . . . Now!'

She hung up and rushed over to join the others. Lucy's eyes were open and stared wildly at them. Her dress was torn and smudged with dirt. She was wearing only one shoe and her other foot was red and swollen. Her hair was bedraggled and her skin was deathly pale.

Teddy grabbed a cushion and made a pillow for her on the floor. As he set her head down, it rolled to one side. There, on the girl's neck, were two dark puncture marks. They were spaced perhaps three or four centimetres apart and purplish-black where the blood had collected and dried.

'They're the same marks!' Greeny cried. 'The exact same marks Juliet had.'

There was silence in the café until finally the little boy spoke. He gulped some water, set down the glass and shuddered.

'It's the vampire. He's come back.'

CHAPTER IV

'VAMPIRE OR NO vampire, I said the party goes ahead!' Richard Stone was not one to mince words, nor to let the small matter of a vampire on the loose interfere with the opening of the Cave. As Ella followed Teddy and his father to the night-club's entrance, she couldn't help thinking about Lucy Vale and Juliet Partridge. There would be no party for them tonight.

'Isn't this exciting?' Rowena Stone said, following behind Ella. Ella smiled back at Teddy's mother, nodding.

She passed through the entrance and caught sight of the passage ahead. A green light exposed the slimy walls. She was surprised that they hadn't tried to disguise the natural setting. As she drew nearer, she reached out her fingers to touch the slime. She laughed, realizing that it was a brilliant fake. She should have known.

Just then, a spray of mist enveloped her and Teddy drew her towards him. Unable to see more than a few paces in front of her, Ella walked on through the passage until the mist swirled away and she found herself at the top of a spiralling stairway, plummeting through the rock.

She followed Teddy on to the stairway, turning briefly to glimpse Rowena's and Ashley's excited faces as they too emerged from the mist. There was the sound of running water ahead. Ella looked down and saw that Teddy was about to be soaked by a waterfall.

'Wait!' she called, but he was already beneath the stream. Miraculously, the water avoided him, flowing into the rock on the other side. Ella walked beneath the spray and found that she too was untouched by the water.

She hurried on down the twisting stairway, catching up with Teddy and his father at the bottom. They were engulfed in another strand of mist.

'Impressed?' asked Richard Stone. As he spoke, he stepped to one side. The mist dissolved and Ella gasped. They were standing in a vast cavern. She had hardly had a chance to take it in, when dance music suddenly began to play and lights started to spin, high up in the roof.

'I've never seen anything like it, Dad!' Teddy said.

Rowena, Ashley and Scott had caught them up. The other guests were close behind. As people arrived in the cavern, there were gasps of appreciation, followed by laughter. The Stones had done it again.

'Let's dance!' Teddy cried, pulling Ella towards the centre of the dance-floor. Ashley and Scott followed.

As she began to move, Ella felt the pounding music pulse through her. The lights seemed to orbit around them, the multi-coloured beams reflected in Teddy's eyes. A strobe came on and Ella was shocked by how it transformed everyone. In the broken light, even Teddy and Ashley's smooth features seemed strange and sinister.

Richard and Rowena Stone joined them on the dance-floor, encouraging the other guests to follow. Ella glanced around, feeling dizzy from the noise and the lights and the endless flow of bodies. She was grateful when the music came to an end. Everyone started to cheer. She turned and saw that Richard Stone had a microphone in his hand. When the cheering subsided, he began to speak.

'Hi, everybody. Thanks for coming. This is a very special night for Smugglers' Cove and for the Stone family. They said we couldn't do it! Well, they were wrong. We *did* do it! Now, let's get the music back on and let's party!'

There were more cheers as the music and flashing lights came on again. Richard Stone rejoined his family.

'Well done, darling!' Rowena said, kissing her husband on the cheek.

'You know it almost didn't happen,' Richard Stone said, frowning.

'What do you mean, Daddy?' Ashley inquired.

'It's this vampire nonsense!' her father replied.

'I had a call from the police this morning. People are saying there should be a curfew in St Dove's. Just when we're ahead of Alton Towers. This is all we need. We're hardly into peak season.'

'You know Lucy Vale hasn't spoken since the attack?' Ashley informed him. 'Just like Juliet. It is kind of scary.'

Richard Stone cut her dead with a glance. 'I don't know what happened to those girls, but I do know this: there's no such thing as vampires.'

There was an awkward silence. Ella glanced away, her eyes sweeping across the sea of dancers. There, at the foot of the stairway, was Alex. His eyes met hers and they walked towards each other, meeting at the edge of the dance-floor.

'Hi,' Alex said.

'I'm glad you came,' Ella said. 'I didn't think you would.'

'I'm sorry.'

'What for?'

'If I've seemed rude to you, or your friends. I guess I'm still in shock . . .'

'It's OK,' Ella said. 'Really! I know how hard it is to settle in a new place. And believe me, St Dove's takes quite a bit of getting used to.'

'Have you lived here long?' Alex asked.

'Greeny and I only moved down last year. From London.' Ella waited for him to ask another question but he didn't. 'So you see, Alex,' she continued, 'I've been there. I know what you're going through.'

He said nothing. His face seemed closed to her again.

'Come on.' She grabbed his arm. 'Let's get a drink.'

They stood at a corner of the bar, drinking Cokes in silence. Around them, there was a hum of chatter as the rest of St Dove's caught up on the gossip and exchanged views on the 'vampire' attacks.

'Do you really think there is a vampire in St Dove's?' Alex asked suddenly. The strength of his stare was unsettling.

'I don't know what I think,' Ella said carefully. 'I mean, we saw the marks on Lucy. What do *you* think?'

He shrugged. 'I think sometimes our eyes deceive us. We see one thing when in fact the truth is quite different.'

Was he trying to tell her something about himself, about his life? Ella tried to get her mind around the riddle but made no headway. She was about to ask him what he meant, when he spoke again.

'It's time I was going.'

'But you've only just arrived,' she protested. He was slipping away from her again, just when she had thought she was getting closer.

'I think your boy-friend wants you,' Alex said.

Ella glanced at Teddy out of the corner of her eye, signalling to her from the middle of the crowd. She turned to say goodbye to Alex but he had already gone. She looked over towards the stairs. Unable to stop herself, she moved through the crowd and started to climb the stairway.

She could hear the echo of his steps just ahead of her as she moved up through the falling water and swirling mist, back to the entrance. The bouncer quickly extinguished a cigarette and nervously dusted himself down.

'Hello, Miss Ryder. Having fun?'

Ella ignored him and carried on, into the darkness, her eyes ranging left and right. She could see no sign of Alex. Suddenly, she heard an engine roar into action. She turned, unable to pinpoint the direction of the sound. Then, out of the darkness, Alex's motor bike came flying towards her.

'Alex, wait!'

He seemed neither to hear nor see her. He drove on past. She ran after him but it was no use. He was already through the theme-park gates. Ella slowed to a standstill and caught her breath.

'Who are you, Alex Culler?' She heard the words fall from her mouth. 'Who are you and what are you doing in St Dove's?'

LATER THAT NIGHT ...

THE PARTY IS over. The gates to the theme park are closed. And the partygoers get out of their cars and taxis into their beds. They must be tired from all that laughter, all that dancing. I too am tired.

There's a sliver of moonlight tonight, but it barely cuts through the clouds. It's the thinnest of light to find your way home by. It reminds me of something long past . . .

I can hear music. The plucking of strings. Somewhere near. Through the trees? I see! Here he sits, picking at the strings of a guitar. I stop and listen. So, he comes here too, to play his music. It is a perfect place, made more perfect by the darkness and the music. I feel . . . soothed. But I can also feel my hunger stirring. Tonight, it will be easy. Tonight, it will be him.

His fingers lift from the strings and he turns, the shadow of the trees keeping half his face in darkness. He sees me standing there, leaning against the branches.

I compliment him on his music and he smiles. He tells me that the others don't understand. That is why he has come to this place at this hour.

He isn't scared. I feel almost that he wants this. As I draw nearer and steady his neck, he remains still. Tonight, my touch is certain, precise.

I drink. He sits, perfectly still. The guitar is balanced on his lap, his fingers resting on the smooth wood surface. When I am done, I back away. A solitary drop of blood escapes from his neck and spills on to the wood.

I take a handkerchief and wipe it up. Then, I walk away. Behind me, I still seem to hear the music, even though his fingers are still.

CHAPTER V

'GOOD MORNING!' CRIED Ashley Stone as Ella closed the door to the Green Room behind her. Ella's hair was drenched with rain, even though the flat she shared with Greeny was only a hundred metres or so from the café.

'Ashley,' Ella said, 'what are you doing here so early?'

'I wanted to see you.'

Ashley's tone was uncharacteristically cool and calculated. She looked perfectly composed. Ella noticed that Ashley's hair had survived the elements intact and her eyes were so bright you would never have known she had been up until three, dancing the night away with Scott.

'I'll get us some tea,' Ella said, disappearing into the kitchen. Greeny looked over from the stove.

'Good morning, sleepy head!' she laughed. 'Rough night?'

'How long has Ashley Stone been here?' Ella hissed.

'The best part of an hour, I'd say. She was asking me all about Alex before.'

'Where *is* Alex?'

'It's Sunday, remember? He won't be in until this evening.'

Ella decided that she would have to face up to Ashley, whatever it was she wanted. Arming herself with two mugs of tea, she backed out of the kitchen, leaving Greeny to her breakfast orders.

'So, how did you enjoy the party?' Ashley asked Ella as she sat down opposite her.

'Oh, it was great,' Ella said, wishing she could sound more convincing.

'I didn't see you and Teddy together much,' Ashley said.

'Oh?'

'No, in fact, you completely disappeared at one point . . .'

Ella sipped her tea cautiously.

'. . . *after Alex arrived*,' Ashley continued, managing to make the three words sound loaded with meaning.

Ella wasn't in the mood for games. If Ashley wanted a fight, she might as well get it over with.

'What's your point, Ashley?' she said.

'My point?' Ashley gazed up at Ella with her innocent blue eyes. 'I'm just making conversation.'

Ella shook her head. 'I don't think you got yourself out of bed early and sat here for an hour waiting for me just to make conversation.'

'OK.' Ashley set her mug on the table and took a deep breath. 'I think you should know that we're all very concerned about your relationship with Teddy.'

Ella wanted to smile. Ashley sounded like she was representing the United Nations.

'Of course, he's far too proud to mention it himself, but it hurts him to see you with Alex. It makes him look foolish. It makes all of us look rather foolish, don't you think?'

The words were too carefully rehearsed – scripted no doubt by Ashley's mother. Rowena Stone must have decided that Ashley had the best chance of pulling Ella into line.

'I think you're making a mountain out of a molehill, Ashley.'

'Really? Alex walks in and you abandon Teddy and the rest of us, without so much as a word, to be with him. And then you both disappear and when you finally come back, a whole hour later, you seem unable to hold a reasonable conversation. I think we deserve an explanation!'

'If Teddy and I are having some problems, it's up to us to sort them out,' Ella said.

'Quite,' Ashley nodded. 'I think you know what you have to do, don't you?'

With that, she pushed back her chair and wrapped her sweater around her shoulders. She stood up and walked to the door, fishing an umbrella out of the stand.

'It's time to choose,' Ashley said, reaching for the door handle. 'Teddy or Alex?'

She pushed open the umbrella and disappeared out on to the beach. Ella didn't know whether to laugh or cry. She reached for the mug of tea and took a gulp.

'What was all that about, then?' Greeny said, having deposited two plates of bacon and eggs at another table.

Ella shrugged. 'It seems that I've fallen out of favour with the Stones.'

'What have you done, love? You didn't go to the party wearing mismatched shoes, did you?'

Ella would have smiled but she was too angry, too confused. 'Ashley says I have to choose between Teddy and Alex.'

'Oh.' Greeny pulled out a chair and sat down. 'I didn't think it had come to that so soon.'

'It hasn't. At least, I don't think it has. I mean I think it's over between Teddy and me. But I've scarcely spoken two sentences to Alex since we met.'

'Maybe Ashley Stone has looked into her crystal ball and seen the future!' Greeny laughed. 'Don't take it too seriously, love. Remember, Ashley's younger than you. If you want my opinion, she's been watching too many soap operas. You'll sort this out with Teddy . . . and Alex. In your own time.'

Greeny reached out and squeezed Ella's shoulder. Ella smiled. She felt better, but it was still a rough way to start the day.

*

Greeny sent Ella back to the flat to get a proper rest. The clouds were beginning to clear. Greeny was right, Ella decided. Ashley *was* a queen of melodrama. Perhaps her visit was simply a misguided attempt to support her big brother. Having gained a better perspective on everything, Ella found it easier to rest and soon drifted off into a smooth, untroubled sleep.

She was woken by a hammering beneath her window. She leaped up and looked through the glass. Teddy was standing below. She drew back, her heart racing. Had he seen her? What did he want? Trying to calm down, she walked through the hallway and down the stairs to the door. He had just started to knock again, when she pulled open the door.

'What's the matter?' she asked.

He said nothing, staring at her with wild eyes. At first, she thought he was angry. Then, she realized that it wasn't that. He looked as if he had had a terrible shock.

'You'd better come in,' she said, pulling him lightly across the threshold and closing the door behind him. She led him into the kitchen.

'Greeny sent me,' he stammered. 'I have some bad news.'

'OK, tell me!'

'There's been another attack,' he said, his face quite expressionless. 'This time it was a boy.'

CHAPTER VI

TEDDY REACHED OVER to pull her towards him, but she resisted.

'Who?' was all she said.

'Chris Kamen,' Teddy said, his expression changing from shock to scorn. 'You know the singer from that local band ... the Disenfranchised ...'

'The Disenchanted,' Ella corrected.

'That's right! Hippy twaddle. Have you got anything to drink?' He opened the refrigerator and pulled out a can. He offered one to Ella, but she shook her head.

'Is he going to be all right?' she asked.

'There were complications this time,' said Teddy, flicking up the ring-pull. 'He was out all night in the rain. They're keeping him at the hospital.'

Ella was silent. She felt uncomfortable at him being here. She knew she was going to have to face him sooner or later, but to have him drag her out of bed like this, with this news.

'Great party last night!' Teddy said, apparently unaware of her unease. 'I swear my dad's a genius. Have you ever seen anything like the Cave before?'

'Teddy, we have to talk.'

'We are talking.' He drained the can.

'I mean talk about us,' she said, fiddling with the belt of her dressing-gown.

'My favourite subject!' he said, smiling. Catching the seriousness of her expression, the smile faded and was replaced by a frown. 'What's up, Ella?'

How could she put these feelings into words? She didn't want to hurt him. But she couldn't go on pretending that nothing had changed.

'I think it's over, Teddy.'

'What?' He looked more astonished than anything else.

'I don't want to go out with you any more.' She had to keep it simple, straightforward.

'Is this about these attacks, this "vampire"?'

'No.'

'But everything was perfect, *is* perfect.'

'No, Teddy,' Ella persisted. Was he really that blind or was he just refusing to accept the truth?

'I've never wanted anything . . . anyone, the way I want you,' he said. Maybe he really thought it was true.

'But I don't want you.' She hadn't meant it to sound so harsh, so final. As the words left her mouth, she could see she had dealt him a fatal blow. He looked devastated.

'I know what this is about,' he said, a nasty edge creeping into his voice. 'It's about Alex, isn't it? You're getting rid of me so you're free for him!'

Ella shook her head. She wasn't about to go into her feelings for Alex with Teddy.

'Well, go right ahead!' he snapped angrily. 'See what a great time you have with Mr Mystery.'

He charged out of the kitchen and raced down the stairs towards the door. Ella followed. What could she say to calm him down?

'Just be careful,' he said as he reached the door. 'You don't know anything about him. For all you know, he could be the vampire.'

With that, he opened the door and slammed it hard behind him. Ella clung to the banisters and collapsed in a heap, fighting back tears. It took her a moment to realize that they were tears of relief.

'That new young doctor from the hospital was in tonight,' Greeny said, carrying a stack of dirty plates into the kitchen. 'Apparently Chris's condition has stabilized.'

'Thank goodness,' Ella sighed.

'What about *your* condition?' Greeny said, checking on a pan of soup. 'How are we going to sort you out, eh?'

Ella took another carrot from the colander and started chopping it.

'You don't have to do that, love,' Greeny said. 'Alex and I are all right, aren't we?'

Alex flipped a couple of burgers over on the grill and nodded. Ella wished that he would say something to comfort her. After all, this was partly his fault. If he hadn't made such a hasty exit from the party . . . If he hadn't come to St Dove's in the first place . . . But it was no use. She couldn't stay angry with him.

'You know what I'd really like?' she said, suddenly brightening. 'A ride on the Harley!'

'Any time!' Alex said, slipping the burger into a bun and spooning barbecue sauce on top.

'How about right now?' Ella said, setting down the knife on the chopping board.

'Done!' Greeny declared. 'It's pretty quiet tonight. I think I can cope on my own.'

'OK,' Alex said, washing his hands. 'We'll drive down the coast. There's somewhere I'd like to show you, Ella.'

Minutes later, they were riding along the coast road. Ella had her arms wrapped tightly around Alex's waist. She had given over all her trust to him. She had no control. They were both wearing helmets so it was difficult to speak to each other, but that suited Ella just fine. She wasn't in the mood for talking. It was the speed she had craved and she wasn't disappointed.

She lost track of how far they travelled. The scenery seemed hardly to change except for the undulations of the cliffs. To start with, she noted the names of the towns as they entered and left them. After a while, she was happy not to know where they were.

Finally, Alex drew the bike to a halt. It was like coming to the end of a brilliant fairground ride. Ella felt a sudden sense of loss as the speed died away.

'Come with me,' Alex said. 'The best views are from up here.'

He didn't wait for her and she had to run to catch him up as he headed across the green to the cliff. As she reached the edge, she gasped. The sun was just about to sink below the horizon and the sea was dark, save for the last golden shards of daylight, floating away.

Ella sat down beside Alex on a rock. He seemed content just to watch the sinking of the sun in silence. She turned her eyes out to sea and let the flickering of the light on the waves carry her away. So, this was what he saw when he looked out to the ocean.

She must have drifted off to sleep. When she came to, she realized that her head was resting on his shoulder. Embarrassed, she pulled away and stood up. Beyond the cliff was only darkness now. She might have been standing at the edge of the world.

'Ready to go back?' he asked, holding out his hand to help guide her through the darkness to where they'd left the bike.

The journey back seemed to take only half as long. Before she knew it, they were retracing their route along the cliff road that led down into St Dove's. If only they hadn't come back so soon. She could have happily driven all through the night.

Suddenly, the bike started to judder. Alex brought the Harley to a standstill. Then he tugged off his helmet.

'Damn! I knew I should have filled up with gas before we came back.'

It was an easy enough mistake to make, but where did it leave them? It wasn't far into town, but the bike was too heavy to push. They couldn't leave it there.

'You go down and get some petrol,' Ella said. 'I'll wait here.'

Alex shook his head. 'I'm not leaving you here.'

'I'll be fine, honestly.'

He gave her a disbelieving look.

'We'll just have to wait here until someone drives past. What time is it?'

'Nearly eleven. Greeny will be tearing her hair out.'

'Someone will come along soon.'

They waited by the side of the road. The moon gave them some light and it was a warm night. All in all, thought Ella, things could have turned out a lot worse.

'Alex?'

'Yes.'

'Why did you come to St Dove's?'

Finally, the question she had been burning to ask since she had first seen him.

'I had to get away.

'From what? And why here?'

He sighed and seemed to be searching for the right words. But before he could speak, they heard the sound of a distant engine. Someone was coming down the road. Alex ran over to attract the driver's attention. The car came into view, a red MG, slowing as it reached Alex. Ella looked across and saw, with a sinking feeling, Ashley and Scott in it. Ashley shot Ella a killer look and whispered something in Scott's ear. They laughed and Scott pushed down hard on the accelerator and drove away.

Alex turned to Ella. She shrugged. It would have been worse to have to accept help from them, she supposed.

'You were saying,' she said, trying to pick up the thread of their conversation, 'why you had to come here.'

'Yes?' Alex looked distracted. Clearly he wanted to keep his attention on the road.

'It's OK if you don't want to tell me,' Ella said.

Alex turned to her, his face bleached white by the moonlight. His eyes burned with a strange intensity.

'My parents died. OK?' And then, before she had the chance to recover from the first shock, 'Actually, they were murdered.'

His eyes bore straight into hers. She was still

grappling with the impact of what he had said. She had created some sort of fantasy around him, without thinking that the secret he was carrying could be something so terrible.

'I'm sorry,' Alex said, suddenly agitated. 'I didn't mean to upset you. Look, could you just stay here for a minute or two? I think . . . I just . . . need to be alone.'

He slipped into the shadows and, in an instant, was gone.

LATER THAT NIGHT ...

SUDDENLY, I KNOW what I need. I'm not sure how much time I have or where I will find it, but there is no alternative.

First, I must get away from here. I move quickly through the darkness. And then, I see it, hidden under the cover of the trees. The red MG. I can't help smiling. It is a perfect solution.

I slow my movements as I approach the car. It is empty. They must be near by. I carry on.

I must focus. Time is short. They are close now, I can feel it. They must be near the cliff-edge. I push on through the trees until I see them. They are together. That was to be expected. I shall have to divide them. Who shall I choose?

I rustle the branches to let them know I'm there.

'What was that?' That's her.

'Where?' Him.

They pull away from each other.

'Wait here!' he tells her.

As he comes towards me, I give him the slip. He disappears into the trees as I emerge from them, ready to surprise her. I'm behind her now and she hasn't even seen me. I reach out and clamp my hand over her mouth.

I clear the hair away from her flesh and move my mouth towards the vein. She puts up a struggle. I am impressed. Then, I manage to restrain her and bury my lips in her neck.

I feel her resistance draining away. She grows limp so that I am holding her up now. I could go on for ever, tonight. But I have to go, to return to the place where I am expected. I can explain a brief disappearance but nothing more.

And so, I leave her. Just in time.

'There's nothing to worry about. There's no one . . .'

I hear his words. I would love to stay and watch his reaction but I must get back. I hear his scream slice through the air. I smile. I can't help myself.

CHAPTER IV

As THE SCREAM finally faded into silence, Ella heard the sound of branches snapping. Alex ran out into the road, panting heavily.

'Alex! Are you OK? Was that you?'

He was unable to speak but he shook his head.

'But look, you're bleeding!'

Still without speaking, he followed her gaze to his shoulder where there was a smear of red. He touched his fingers to the wound at the base of his neck and saw the red on his fingertips.

'It's nothing,' he said, huskily. 'I scraped against a branch.'

Ella began to walk over to him. He turned away. They both froze as they heard the sound. An engine. They looked up the road. A pair of headlights swooped down, almost blinding them. As the shock of the light receded, Ella turned and signalled to the truck to stop. The truck drove up to them and slowed to a standstill. The driver, a boy of Alex's age, leaned out of the window.

'Are you in some kind of trouble?' he inquired.

'My bike broke down,' Alex said. 'Could you give us a lift into St Dove's?'

'Sure!' said the driver. 'I'll give you a hand to load the bike in the back.' As he stepped down from the truck, he held out his hand.

'Mike Morgan.'

Alex and Ella introduced themselves as they climbed up beside Mike on to the bench seat at the front of the truck.

'You play in the Disenchanted, don't you, Mike?' Ella said.

He nodded, starting up the engine.

'You know what happened to Chris?'

'How's he doing?' Alex asked.

'Not too good,' Mike replied.

'I'm sorry,' Ella said.

'I think he'll pull through,' Mike went on, adjusting the rear view mirror. 'In the mean time, we're supposed to be playing at Westonbury this weekend. Question is, can we find ourselves a new singer?'

There was silence.

'That sounds awful, doesn't it?' Mike said, his tone of voice changing. 'I mean, he's my best friend and I'm fretting about some gig. It's just . . . we've been working towards this for the past two years. We were finally getting it together . . . and now this. He'd want us to be there. I know he would.'

He shook his head. 'That's why I was up here. I was waiting . . . to catch the vampire. Crazy, huh? But the vampire has struck three times on this stretch.'

Ella looked over at Alex but he was staring coolly out of the window. She shivered.

'I don't know what I was thinking of. It's a good thing you guys came along. I'd have probably ended up as the next victim –' Mike turned to Alex – 'if I hadn't heard you scream.'

'I didn't scream,' Alex said.

Mike's jaw dropped and a curious expression took over his face.

'Then, who?'

'Mike, slow down! Look!' Ella cried.

Mike stamped his foot on the brake before looking out to see the figure standing in the middle of the road, waving his arms frantically.

'Another breakdown?' Mike said, slowing the truck.

'I don't think so,' Ella said as Scott ran over to the window. His hair was dishevelled and his shirt and jeans were torn and stained with dirt . . . and blood.

'You've got to help!' he yelled. 'Please help me! It's Ashley. She's been attacked.'

Ella thought Scott was going to tear the door off the truck. But when he realized they were going to help, he turned and disappeared into the trees.

Minutes later, he returned, carrying Ashley in his arms. Ella gasped. Ashley lay there, limp as a rag doll, her long blonde curls matted and out of shape. Her arms dangled lifelessly, as pale as china. And there, at the base of her neck, were the tell-tale marks.

'They're going to kill me,' Scott said to Ella. 'You know what they're like.'

In spite of herself, she felt sorry for him. He'd been scared half to death by the attack on Ashley and now he would have to tell her parents what had happened. As Mike drove the truck up the driveway to the Stones' house, Scott began to panic.

'Ella, won't you come in? You could help. You know them.'

She shook her head. 'It would only make things worse. You know how they feel about me right now. I'm the last person they want to see.'

And so Scott carried Ashley out into the darkness alone. The others watched from the truck as he approached the front door. It opened and lights flooded the windows. Ella caught sight of Teddy running out to help Scott. Richard Stone was close behind, followed by Rowena. In the confusion, none of them seemed to notice the truck pull away down the drive.

'I'll take you guys home,' Mike said.

They came to Alex's house first and he and Mike lifted down the Harley. As they did so, Alex said, 'This probably isn't the right time, but I used to sing in a band at home.'

'Great!' said Mike. 'We're rehearsing at my place tomorrow . . . I mean later this morning. Why don't you come over?'

Ella listened to Mike giving Alex instructions on how to get to his house. At least something good had come out of all the madness.

'Good-night!' Alex called out to her. He seemed brighter than before.

'Good-night!' she called back. 'Thanks for the ride.'

The words died on her lips as the front door opened and an old man appeared. His face was lined and he was frowning. He said something to Alex. Ella couldn't catch the words but he seemed to be angry. Alex snapped back and followed the old man inside. The door slammed shut behind them.

'Gabriel Culler looked pretty angry,' Ella said as they drove away.

Mike nodded. 'He certainly did.'

'I've never really seen him up close before.'

'Haven't you been into his shop?' Mike said and continued as Ella shook her head, 'It used to really spook me when I was a kid. All these clocks all over the place. All set at different times. I remember going in there with my dad once and this cuckoo shot right out at my ear. I had to be carried away, screaming.'

He laughed at the memory. Ella found herself laughing with him, welcoming this release from the tension.

'Of course,' Mike said, 'Culler will be in his element now.'

'What do you mean?' Ella could see the Green Room up ahead and, beyond, the flat. A light was on in her bedroom window.

'Haven't you heard the stories?' Mike said, halting the truck.

'What stories?'

'Well, apparently, old Gabriel Culler is an expert on vampires.'

Ella thanked Mike and wandered up the path to the flat. The events of the evening ran through her head like a videotape on fast forward. Certain moments, certain words came back to her. She remembered what Alex had said about his parents being murdered. She heard the scream cutting through the air. She saw the expression on Alex's face as he glanced at the blood on his fingertips. And she saw again Gabriel Culler's anger as he pulled Alex inside. And, through it all, the same question pounded away inside her head. If Gabriel Culler was an expert on vampires, who or what was Alex?

CHAPTER VIII

THE NEXT MORNING, Ella woke to find that Greeny had already left the flat. She dressed quickly and hurried to the Green Room. She found her in the kitchen, furiously chopping up vegetables for a soup.

'I think you owe me an explanation,' Greeny snapped.

Ella saw that her eyes were bright with tears. Clearly, she was more upset than angry.

'I was so scared,' she said, letting go of the knife. 'I thought . . . I thought . . .' But her mouth refused to make the words.

'I know,' Ella said, going over to hug her. 'I know. I had no right to do that to you. Things just got out of hand.'

She relayed to Greeny the strange events of the previous night, omitting a few details that she thought would only upset her further. Greeny listened attentively. When Ella stopped speaking, Greeny was silent.

'Well?' Ella prompted.

'What can I say? I don't understand any of this. I never believed in vampires. I still don't know what to think. I don't know how we can protect ourselves. All I do know is I'm very scared.'

Ella reached over and hugged Greeny again. They held each other close for a while.

'What's all this then?' Alex said, striding into the café, followed by Mike and the other two members of the Disenchanted.

'Hi, Alex,' Ella said, turning. 'Well, Mike, did he make the grade?'

'He was fantastic,' Mike replied, looking in awe at Alex.

Alex looked embarrassed and busied himself introducing Patrick, the bass player, and Steve, the drummer.

'I need a favour,' Alex said to Greeny. 'Could I have Saturday night off to go to Westonbury?'

'Well, Saturday night is our busiest time, you know. And I'm not sure I approve of all that *loud* music . . . of course you can!' she laughed. 'I wouldn't let you miss this chance for anything, my love.'

Later, when Mike and the other guys from the band drove off home, Alex and Ella went for a stroll along the beach.

'It's good to see you making a life for yourself here in St Dove's,' Ella said.

'It's all thanks to you.'

'What do you mean?' Ella asked, turning and brushing a strand of hair from her eyes.

'Well, if you hadn't wanted to go for a ride last night, we'd never have got stuck on the cliff. And Mike would never have stopped to help us and so I'd never have found out that the band was looking for a singer!'

'I'm not so sure.'

Alex looked at Ella quizzically.

'Don't you believe in fate? That some things are just meant to happen? That however you try, whatever you do, you can't force them and you can't stop them.'

As they walked on, Alex seemed to be considering the proposition.

'I suppose I feel I could have stopped my parents' murder,' he said at last.

He still hadn't told her any more about what had happened and Ella wouldn't push him. Her curiosity about him had changed into something deeper, stronger.

Suddenly, Alex stopped walking. He faced Ella squarely and reached out his arms until they rested on her shoulders. Then, as if in slow motion, he leaned in close and his mouth met hers. He kissed her, gently, on the lips. As he pulled away, she looked up at him in surprise.

'What was that for?'

'For taking some of the guilt away,' Alex said. 'I don't know whether I believe in fate. But I do believe in you.'

This time, she pulled him towards her and they kissed for longer. Alex's eyes closed and Ella closed hers too, letting herself float away on the delicious sensation.

When they drew away again, they joined

hands and walked out towards the ocean, coming to a standstill at the water's edge. Ella could feel Alex grow tense. She saw that his eyes were fixed on the foam that travelled across the sand, ending its journey just in front of their feet.

'I've not been this near water since –' Alex broke off.

Ella watched as another wave came in towards them.

'My parents . . . they died at sea,' he said.

'You were with them?' Ella said, suddenly understanding.

'Yes. I was on the boat. But I escaped. I had to –'

'It's OK, you don't have to tell me.'

'No, I want to! I had to escape because I had to save my brother.'

Ella looked at him in shock. This was the first time he had mentioned a brother. She followed his gaze out into the churning surf, sensing his despair.

'But you couldn't save him, Alex, could you? He's dead too, isn't he?'

Slowly Alex turned away from the water and dropped his head.

'As good as,' he mumbled.

They walked back across the beach, hand in hand. Just when his mood had seemed to be lifting, the thought of his brother had depressed him again. Ella found herself full of more questions. Who was this brother? What had happened to him? If he wasn't dead, where was he now? But she couldn't ask Alex any of this, not yet.

As they were nearing the Green Room, Ella saw the familiar outline of Teddy's VW parked on the cliff. Scott's MG slid into view beside it. Teddy came over and stood at the cliff-edge, staring down at Alex and Ella. Ella could feel Alex start to release her hand, but she gripped him all the more tightly. He looked at her questioningly but, ignoring his gaze, she walked on.

By the time they reached the café, Teddy, Scott and Jeff had climbed down the steps. Ella and Alex turned as Teddy strode over.

'Ashley's condition is stable, thanks for asking,' he said, sarcastically.

'We're forming a search party,' Scott said.

'There's a whole lot of kids meeting down here later,' Jeff added. 'We're going to stake out the cliff-top.'

'The vampire has attacked there four times,' Ella said. 'Aren't you afraid you'll be setting yourselves up for the next victim?'

'Will you join us?' Jeff asked.

Ella looked at Alex and then back at the three others.

'We can't come tonight,' Ella said. 'We have to work here.'

'But afterwards?' Jeff persisted. 'We're going to stay up there all night!'

Ella shook her head. 'No. I'm not coming,' she said, moving towards the door of the café.

'What about you, Alex?' Teddy said.

Ella stopped dead in her tracks, turning to see Teddy stand before Alex, his arms folded tightly across his chest. 'You were there last night. You saw what happened to my sister. Will you come and help us stop it happening again?'

Alex didn't reply. He seemed to be looking through Teddy. Ella wondered if he was thinking again of his family, the family he had lost.

'If you're not with us, then you're against us,' said Teddy.

'You would say that,' Ella snapped, angrily. 'That's the way everything works with you. Everything's black or white. Well, it's not that simple, Teddy. It's not that simple. When are you going to get that into that sunburned skull of yours?'

She reached out her hand to Alex, but it was Teddy who grabbed it, seizing her by the wrist and spinning her back to face him. She could feel his hot breath on her face as he began to speak.

'You've changed, you know. You used to be sweet and kind and –'

'No. No, Teddy. I'm no different to how I always was. Perhaps you're just seeing me for real at last. And perhaps I'm seeing you for what you are too.'

LATER THAT NIGHT . . .

THE MADNESS HAS begun again. It always does, no matter how far I travel. It is as inescapable as the hunger.

They are up at the top of the cliffs now, torches in hand. They think they are the first, but I have been here before with other crowds. The fear is the same, the panic. When will I learn that this is something to be afraid of? That I am something to be afraid of?

Even if I hadn't heard in advance of their plans, they would not have tricked me. I shall not walk along the cliff path tonight. There are other paths, other ways . . .

I look over now as the cliffs melt into the distant sky, the moonlight lapping at their edge. I was happy here. Where will I go next? Where is there left to go?

I see the hospital ahead of me. There's a nurse leaving. As she drives off, I walk into the car-park. A sign up ahead tells me what I need to know.

Hospital corridors are the same the world over. The same lino that makes your shoes click in a certain way, the same smell.

It's ridiculously easy to get to where I need to

go. The door, of course, is locked but a moment later, I am on the other side. I'm surrounded by refrigerators. Which shall I choose? What does it matter? I pull open a door and stare at the row of glass bottles. Maybe I should have done this earlier. Maybe then I could have avoided all the madness.

As I walk back through the darkness, I am overwhelmed with melancholy. I have satisfied that hunger but a different one remains. I look up to the cliffs. The torches are still shining.

I look down to the beach. I glimpse a boy and girl walking hand in hand by the edge of the ocean. It makes me unbearably sad. I look away. When I look back again, they have disappeared.

CHAPTER IX

ELLA SAT BY the window, turning the pages of the newspaper without really taking in any of the information. The world seemed a faraway place. All that mattered was what was happening in St Dove's. She felt her world was marked out by Teddy on one side and Alex on the other. It was an uncomfortable place to be.

Alex had set off early for Westonbury with Mike and the others to get ready for their performance that evening. He'd gone to Mike's to rehearse after his shift in the café the night before. They had said Ella could sit in but she had decided to wait to see them up on the stage. She was both excited and scared for Alex.

Gazing through the window, she saw that the beach was empty. It was rare for there to be no early morning surfers or walkers. Perhaps the rest of St Dove's was exhausted from the night before. Even Greeny was sleeping in. Ella felt like she had the whole town to herself.

Folding up the newspaper, she came to a decision. She grabbed an apple from the bowl on the counter and headed out of the Green Room, locking it behind her.

The air was brisk, if not quite chill and Ella was glad she had brought a sweater. She realized with a shock that it was an old cricket sweater of Teddy's. For a moment, her blood ran cold. Then she decided not to be silly. She could return it to him later.

She walked up the cliff path, not encountering a soul, and took the fork that led into town. The high street was empty too. The shops were shut up, with 'closed' signs hung behind the glass doorways. She came to a stop in front of a shop-window, noticing a light inside.

Ella rang the bell and waited. There was a 'closed' sign here too, but that didn't matter. She knew he was there. She rang the bell again and rapped on the window-pane. Soon she heard footsteps.

The door opened. He didn't look surprised to see her. His lined face scarcely made any expression as he held the door open for her.

'I thought it would be you,' he said, somewhat irritably. 'I knew you'd come, sooner or later.'

Ella stepped inside and he locked the door behind her. Her eyes darted around the room, from one clock-face to another. She could see why Mike had been scared as a child. There was something forbidding about all the old clocks, as if they sat in judgement of her. They seemed to hiss at her as she walked past them.

'Come this way, Miss Ryder,' Gabriel Culler said, leading her into a workshop at the back.

Ella stood before a long desk, littered with bits and pieces of old clocks and watches, tools and rags. Culler lifted an ornate carriage clock off a chair and indicated to her to sit.

'You've been seeing quite a bit of Alex.'

Ella nodded. 'We've become friends.'

'Have you now,' said Culler, picking up a small wristwatch and dropping it into his palm.

'He's told me about his parents, and his brother.'

'Oh.' Culler still refused to be surprised.

'I need to know more,' Ella said. 'You must see that. I want to help him but I have to know more. And I can't ask him. That's why I'm here.'

Culler moved the silver watch around in his palm, weighing her words.

'All right, Miss Ryder,' he said, at last, 'I'll tell you what you want to know. But first, there's something I must ask you.'

He looked up into her eyes. She quivered. He had exactly the same eyes as Alex.

When Ella got back to the Green Room, she saw that Greeny had opened up. Scott and Jeff were sitting, drinking coffee, by the window.

'How did the stake-out go?' she asked them.

Their eyes met hers but neither of them spoke. Frowning, she turned away and saw Greeny, standing in front of the kitchen door. There was a strange expression on her face.

'Come in here,' she said.

Ella followed her into the kitchen. Something important had obviously happened, but what?

As she entered the kitchen she saw Teddy sitting at the table. He was pale and drawn in a black turtleneck. She was used to seeing him in bright T-shirts. He looked older suddenly.

'I think you should sit down,' Greeny said, pulling out a chair for herself.

'Would someone tell me what's going on?' Ella said, leaning against the counter.

Teddy looked sombrely at Greeny. She nodded. Carefully, he pulled down the turtleneck. There, at the base of his neck, were two small holes in his flesh, ringed with dried blood. His neck was red and raw.

'No!' Ella cried. 'No. It's not possible.'

Greeny reached out a hand to steady her, but Ella shook it off.

'I don't believe it!' she said, but the wound seemed real enough. 'All right, I've seen enough. Get out of here.'

Teddy walked out of the kitchen without looking behind him.

Ella found herself crying. 'I don't understand,' she said, burying her head in her hands. 'I just don't understand.'

'It happened on the cliffs,' Greeny said calmly. 'The usual place. Teddy had heard something. He wandered away from the search party, through some bushes into a clearing. He realized his mistake but it was too late. Thankfully, the others quickly saw that he was missing and found him. He was unconscious, but they rushed him home and he made a quick recovery. They decided to call off the search party.'

Ella heard the words but she couldn't let them take hold.

'Last night,' Greeny continued, 'Ashley Stone began talking about what happened to her. The last thing she remembered seeing was Alex, in the bushes.'

'It isn't him. He isn't the vampire!' Ella sobbed.

Greeny wrapped her arms around her.

'It's hard to accept, love, of course it is —'

'No!' Ella pushed her away and ran out of the kitchen.

As she ran out of the café, Teddy darted up from his chair. Ella went on to the beach, towards the sea. She could feel Teddy running behind her, closing the gap. She ran on, losing momentum, until she came to the water's edge. He was level with her now and grabbed her, spinning her round to face him.

'You *have* to believe this,' he said, 'for your own sake if nothing else. How do you know he won't attack you? No one is safe until he leaves St Dove's. No one.'

The wind dried the tears on Ella's face and he held her as her breathing started to slow.

'It all makes sense,' Teddy said. 'It all fits, like

a jigsaw. The attack on Juliet happens just before he shows up. Then, bingo, he gets her job in the café. Then Chris Kamen gets attacked and Alex just happens to be available to take his place in the band –'

'You're forgetting Lucy Vale,' Ella interrupted. 'What was his motive for that?'

'It's the exception that proves the rule,' Teddy said, still holding her tightly. 'You were up on the cliffs the night Ashley was attacked. You know it had to be Alex. And then last night, he attacked me. It's not hard to figure out why, is it?'

Ella didn't answer.

'Because he knew you were going to come back to me. OK, so we needed a break from each other. I can see that now. But you were always going to come back. I knew that. And he did too.'

Ella felt the rush of tears seizing her again. She was so confused by this. If only Alex were there. If only he could speak up for himself.

'It's all right,' Teddy said, drawing her towards him. 'It's all right. It's nearly over. You're safe now . . . as long as you stay away from him.'

Ella pulled away, seeing clearly at last. 'That's why you're doing this! To try to keep me away from him. That's all that matters to you. You'll stop at nothing!'

She turned and marched back across the

beach. She was going to Westonbury. She didn't care what Teddy Stone claimed. She was going to Westonbury. She was going to Alex.

CHAPTER X

A S THE TRAIN pulled into Westonbury station, Ella glanced at her watch. Just after six. The Disenchanted were due on stage in half an hour. There were hoards of people heading towards the concert site and she would have to hurry to make it on time. She tightly clutched the ticket Alex had given her as she jostled through the crowd. It was twenty-five past six once she found a space close to the edge of the stage.

'Watch it!' a girl snapped. 'We've been here since five!'

'Let her stay,' her boy-friend said, smiling at Ella.

Ella smiled back and took her place. Music was blasting from the loudspeakers. Sun blazed down on to the crowd and the friendly boy next to her offered Ella a can of Coke. She accepted it gratefully, enjoying the disapproving looks from the girl. Get a life! Ella felt her mood lift. She felt defiant. She was sick of people telling her what to do, telling her what was safe and what was dangerous. She was perfectly capable of deciding exactly what she wanted.

Six-thirty passed and the Disenchanted did

not appear on the stage. Six-forty and Ella looked around to find more and more people swarming into the arena. The band couldn't have wished for a better crowd. She felt nervous for them and wondered how Alex must be feeling.

Ella thought that the cheers would deafen her as the band finally made their way on to the stage and picked up their instruments. Mike and Patrick strummed a few practice notes on their guitars. Steve sat down behind his drum-kit. Then, Alex came forward to the microphone.

He looked different to Ella. He was wearing the same clothes as usual, a dark shirt and jeans, but his eyes were covered with sun-glasses. Perhaps that's what it was. Whatever, he seemed more confident on the stage. As he cupped his hands around the microphone, the crowd became silent.

'We are . . . the Disenchanted,' he said.

As his words echoed around the arena, the music began and a wave of light shot across the stage. The crowd cheered as Alex began to sing.

He was good. The band was good. Ella found herself swaying along to the music. Looking across the crowd, she saw that everyone was. The atmosphere was electric.

As the last guitar chord brought the first song to an end, the guy beside her turned and shouted over the noise, 'They're brilliant!'

Ella beamed, unable to take her eyes off Alex.

He was drinking thirstily from a bottle of water, apparently immune to the crowd's roars of approval.

Two songs later, the Disenchanted's set came to a close. They took a bow, waved to the audience and reluctantly left the stage. But the cheers were so strong that they had to go back on. Delighted, the boys picked up their instruments and launched into another number. This time, Ella saw even Alex smile at the crowd's reaction.

When they finally left the stage, to the disappointed shouts from the audience, Ella made her way back through the crowd to the side of the stage. A security guard stepped in front of her.

'Where are you going?' she inquired.

'I'm a friend of the band,' Ella said.

'How many times have I heard that?' the woman said, looking at her disbelievingly.

'Really, I am,' Ella said.

'Ella! You made it.'

Over the security guard's shoulder, Mike was waving to her. With a sigh, Ella was let through. She ran over to Mike and gave him a hug.

'You were fantastic!' she cried.

'What about Alex, then?'

Mike put his arm around Ella's shoulder and led her through the maze of wires and trucks backstage. Alex, Patrick and Steve were sitting by some steps, talking to . . . no it couldn't be. But it was. As Ella came closer, she heard the

American rock god tell Alex what a great future he had. As the star walked off back to his entourage, Mike touched Alex on the shoulder.

'Someone to see you,' he said.

Alex turned and stood, framed by the sunshine. Suddenly, Ella felt nervous. He had become something beyond her reach. She felt embarrassed. He removed his sun-glasses, walked over to her and took her, trembling, into his arms, kissing her. She stopped shaking and kissed him back, running her fingers through his hair.

The band made room for Ella, letting her into their camaraderie. They were thrilled with the crowd's reaction and wanted to hear what she had thought about everything. Together, they replayed the performance over and over again. Ella leaned her head on to Alex's shoulder and curled up, comfortably. She didn't care what anyone said. This was where she wanted to be.

'You can't come in here!'

The security guard was having to ward off more would-be visitors. Her words had become a familiar refrain, but this time there was a note of panic in her voice that made Ella and the others turn.

'No! I said NO.'

'What's going on?' Patrick asked.

Then Ella heard a familiar voice.

'Quick! There he is!'

Teddy and Scott came flying over the barrier

as Jeff pushed the guard out of the way. Mike ran to restrain Teddy, but Teddy easily overpowered him, sending him reeling with a punch. Teddy ran on towards Alex. Patrick tried to catch Scott from behind but before he could reach him, Jeff brought him down with a rugby tackle. He fell, catching his ankle in a coil of wires. Steve made a half-hearted attempt to block the others from Alex, but Alex pushed him out of the way, standing defiantly before Teddy, Scott and Jeff.

'Leave my friends alone. It's me you want, isn't it?'

Without speaking, Jeff and Scott grabbed Alex on either side and led him out of the backstage area.

Teddy stood before Ella, calmly folding his arms across his chest. 'I'm doing this for you. I'm saving you from yourself.'

He turned and followed the others, stepping over Patrick as he walked away. As soon as he was out of earshot, Ella turned to Steve.

'We have to follow them,' she said. 'There's no telling what they'll do to him.'

Steve didn't miss a beat, hurrying over to help Patrick out of the tangle. 'We'll take Mike's truck,' he said. 'Don't worry, Ella.'

The roof of Teddy's VW was peeled back and it looked for all the world as if four friends were out for a drive.

Mike was having a hard time keeping up in his truck. He, Ella and Patrick were sandwiched on the front seat, with Steve doing his best to sit still in the back of the truck.

'Where are they taking him?' Steve asked.

Ella began to recognize the route. She said nothing but a sign appeared, confirming her suspicions. *Smugglers' Cove. The authentic Cornish experience.*

They followed the VW as it neared the theme park. Teddy drove past the main gates. He must be going in through the back, Ella thought. Sure enough, he drove on around the park's perimeter until he reached a rough, unlit country road.

Ella had never seen this road before but she could make out the various attractions, silhouetted against the night sky. She saw the galleon, poised forever about to sink, jutting out of the fake harbour. And there was the haunted tin mine, perched on the cliff. Where were they going to take Alex?

Mike stopped the truck and, careful not to make a sound, jumped to the ground. The others followed and approached the black VW. They could hear Teddy shouting instructions.

'This way. Quickly!'

As his voice grew fainter, they ran ahead. They came to a high fence. There was a gate but it was bolted.

'Teddy must have a key,' Mike said, despairingly.

Patrick tried to get a foothold in the fence. He fell backwards and groaned as he hit the ground.

Suddenly, there was an explosion of barking and a dog threw itself at the fence from the other side.

'Who's there? What's going on?' A security guard waved a torch in their faces.

Ella stepped forward.

'I'm Ella Ryder . . . Teddy Stone's girlfriend.' She hated saying the words but it was her only chance. 'He came in through the gate.'

'It's locked,' the guard said, looking at her suspiciously. She hadn't seen him before. Maybe he was new.

'He had a key,' Ella replied.

'Let's get this straight,' the guard said. 'He had a key and let himself in but then he locked it again before you could follow.'

'Something like that,' she said, wishing she had had time to concoct a more likely story.

'I'm not permitted to let anyone into the park after hours, even . . . friends of the Stone family,' the guard sneered. 'You'll have to come back in the morning.'

'No!' Ella said, flinging herself at the fence. 'No!'

Mike reached out and pulled her back. 'It's OK, sir,' he said. 'We understand.'

The guard huffed and called the dog away.

'We can't leave him there,' Ella said. 'They'll kill him.'

'What else *can* we do?' Steve said, dejectedly.

No one spoke. Then, out of the silence came voices, familiar voices.

'That'll keep him out of the way.'

'Now what?'

The key turned in the lock and Ella pushed the others back into the bushes. Teddy stepped through the gate, followed by Scott and Jeff. They walked over to Teddy's car and climbed in. As Teddy started up the engine, Ella heard Scott speak.

'Why don't we just finish him off, now?'

'Just listen to yourself,' snapped Teddy. 'Like some kind of homicidal maniac. I want him out of town just as much as you do, but I'm not going to prison. There has to be another way.'

LATER THAT NIGHT . . .

THE STONE HOUSE is shrouded in darkness. I walk up the driveway, past the VW, and approach the door. It is locked securely but I'm not going to be put off now. In an instant I am standing in the hallway, stepping across the chequered marble tiles.

A long staircase swoops down from above. I begin to climb, pausing on the stairs to look at some of the family photographs that line the walls. Teddy was really quite an ugly child.

I make my way across the landing, then I hear a sound from below. I retrace my steps, noiselessly, and glance down the stairwell. I see Teddy, padding out across the hall, a plate of food in his hand.

As he begins to climb the stairs, I pull back into the shadows. He is coming close now. I hold my breath and let him pass me. He goes a few steps along the corridor and I follow. He stops. I stop. He turns and casually pushes open a door. As I appear inside the room, his mouth falls open.

'What are you doing? How did you . . .' I want to tell him to keep quiet, but he is incapable of saying anything else.

'I wanted to talk to you,' I say, glancing out of the window. I see him eye the doorway, hopefully. I shake my head and move over to block the exit. I'm not about to let him get away. 'What's the matter? Once bitten, twice shy?'

He says nothing. He is shaking all over. I lean forward and inspect the wound. As I thought, it has almost closed.

'You went to some trouble, faking this. It must have been very sore. It's quite convincing – but then you did see the marks on Lucy and Ashley, didn't you?'

'What do you want?' he manages to croak.

'A chance to set the record straight,' I say. 'You see, there was no plan. Not really. It was all pretty random. And I was careful. I never took so much that they wouldn't recover. In a day or so, Juliet and Lucy will start to feel better. They won't remember anything about the attack, and pretty soon life will be back to normal for them. Chris too. Of course, Ashley was found just afterwards so her recovery was quicker. Do you understand what I'm saying? I could have killed them but I chose not to.'

He is incapable of speaking or even nodding. I bend my head towards him.

'You got it wrong, Teddy. You tried to fake it but the joke's on you. Tomorrow morning, when they find you, you'll have real bite-marks to show them . . .'

Chapter XI

THERE WAS NO trick lighting or fake mist as Ella made her way down the spiralling stone stairway this time. Her footsteps echoed against the stone. Other than that, the only sound was her own breathing.

As she reached the bottom of the steps, she flashed the torch around the room. There in the corner, she saw him and ran over to him.

They had bound and gagged him and as Ella pulled the cloth from his mouth, she was relieved to see that he was still able to breathe. His eyes flashed up at her gratefully and he began to speak. She placed a finger over his mouth.

'It's OK,' she said. 'Save your energy. You're going to need it.'

She turned him around and worked at the intricate knots that Scott and Jeff had tied. Finally she freed him, pulling the rope away.

'Come on,' she said. 'There's not much time. It'll be light soon.'

He pulled her back, his arms holding her waist. 'Before we go, there's something I have to tell you.'

'All right, but quick . . .'

This time, it was his turn to hush her. He

waited until he had her full concentration. 'I'm not the vampire. You have to believe me.'

He looked so solemn that she wanted to laugh. 'I do believe you. I always knew it wasn't you.'

She wanted to turn. There was so much to sort out. They had to get going.

'How? How could you be sure?'

'Because *I'm* the vampire.'

The words came out casually but their weight was not lost on him. He drew her towards him and held her in his arms. She was stunned. She had resigned herself simply to rescuing him and then leaving town herself. Nothing more.

'How could I have been so blind? Of course. It makes sense, now.'

'Aren't you scared?'

He shook his head. 'How could I ever be scared of you? I love you, Ella.'

He kissed her on the lips, sweetly. She thought she was going to cry. 'What's the matter?'

She didn't answer. Couldn't he see that it was over? He would go his way and she would go hers. It was always like this. Always, she disappeared without trace, like a sand castle swept away by the tides. It had never been so hard before, not since the beginning. She had never met anyone like Alex.

'It's impossible,' she said. 'We can't be together.'

'Why? I have nothing if I don't have you.'

Did he really mean it? She felt herself resisting. It was her only way of protecting herself. If she dared to believe in this dream, how would she ever recover when it crumbled away like all the others?

'You don't understand,' she said, at last.

'What don't I understand? Tell me.'

'There's so much. I don't know where to begin. But it could never work, you as you are and me as . . . what I am.'

He drew away and tore at the back of his shirt, kneeling in front of her, exposing his neck. 'Then make me the same.'

She looked down at the smooth flesh above his shoulder-bone. It would only take a minute or two. All the years of loneliness would be at an end. Her head was spinning with possibilities.

'No, no. I won't do it,' she said. 'There's so much you don't know. I won't do that to . . . to someone I love.'

'But it would be different. We'd have each other . . .'

She turned away. She had made her decision. It was the right decision, the only decision. He would be grateful to her someday.

Gabriel Culler was waiting when they arrived back at the house.

'I've packed your things, Alex,' he said. 'There's money too. It's time you went home. You're ready now.'

The old man smiled and opened his arms. Alex hugged him.

'Thank you . . . Grandfather . . . for everything.' He turned towards Ella. 'You could come, you know.'

'Alex, we've been through this.'

'Let's go through it again. Why can't you come with me? It's as good a place as any.'

'Maine?' Ella thought for a moment. 'America? All right. Why not?'

Alex burst into a smile and took her in his arms, spinning her around the room. She smiled too, even though her heart was breaking. He might believe that they could carry on like this but she knew that their time was limited. Maybe she could go with him now but one day, not far off, they would have to go their separate ways.

'OK, then. That's agreed. Why don't you go down to the flat and pick up some things . . . Oh, what about Greeny?'

It was as if he had run out of steam. Already, he too was seeing the obstacles that stood in their way.

'I'll tell her it's a holiday,' Ella said. 'I don't want her to know the truth.'

'You're sure?'

She nodded.

'All right then. I'll bring the bike down to the Green Room.'

Alex went into his room to pick up the things Culler had packed for him. Culler led Ella along the hallway and reached for the doorknob. As he did so, there was a hammering on the outside.

'Whatever's that?' the old man said, pulling open the door.

Richard Stone marched in. 'Where is he?'

Ella stepped back along the hallway and into Alex's room. 'They've come for you already. You'll have to go ahead without me. Here's what you must do. Remember where we drove to that night on the bike? Drive there and wait for me. I'll pick up my things from the flat and get Mike to take me to you. Now go!'

Alex leaped out through the back door as Richard Stone pushed Culler out of the way and stormed through the hallway. He found Ella in Alex's room and saw the Harley shoot off along the road.

Stone looked Ella in the eye. 'I won't forget this.'

There was no time to say anything more. He ran back out of the house and into his car. Ella followed and saw that Scott and Jeff were right behind him. Other members of the Stones' trusty circle were behind them. What chance did Alex have? She ran out into the street and all the way to Mike's house.

'You've got to help me,' she said. 'I'll explain as we go.'

They jumped into the truck and Mike started up the engine. Ella was about to tell him to drive

85

to the flat when something made her change her mind.

'Follow the cars,' she cried. 'Try to overtake them. Alex *has* to get away.

Mike rammed his foot down on the accelerator and soon caught up with the car at the back of the pack and overtook it. The cars in front of them were gaining on Alex.

'You'll have to get closer,' Ella said, in desperation. 'They'll be on the cliff road soon, where it's too narrow to overtake.'

She wasn't sure how Mike did it, but he managed to cut ahead of two more cars. Now, there was only Richard Stone's Jaguar and Scott's MG between Alex and them.

Alex surged ahead up the cliff road. Stone followed. Mike tried to overtake Scott's MG but Scott just accelerated.

'Damn!' Mike thumped the wheel.

All they could do now was watch. Ella felt sick to the pit of her stomach. If only Alex could just pull away. She had never wanted anything so much.

But Stone was catching up. They were near the peak of the cliff now. The nose of the Jaguar was almost level with the back of the Harley. Alex turned as the car nudged the back of the bike. As he did so, the bike careered off the road and on to the grass verge. Alex did his best to keep control but the ground was uneven and he was travelling much too fast.

Ella and Mike watched in horror as the Harley hurtled towards the barrier at the edge of the cliff and smashed straight through it. The bike went flying down the cliff, throwing Alex into the sea below and crashing down after him.

'No!' Ella screamed. 'NO!'

One by one the cars drew to a standstill. First the Jaguar, then the MG, then Mike's truck. Stone rushed to the edge of the cliff, followed by Scott and Jeff. Ella jumped down from the truck. Mike tried to stop her but he couldn't.

'I'm so sorry,' Stone cried, his voice now a horrified whisper. 'You have to believe me. I never meant this to happen. It was an accident.'

Ella had nothing to say to him. She turned away and looked down into the sea. There was no trace of the bike or Alex. The waves rolled in on to the beach remorselessly as if it were just another day.

LATER THAT DAY . . .

I STAND AT the ocean's edge, letting the day die around me. There are surfers in the water, fooling around. The waves are not high enough for surfing. Even I know that. I watch them, sitting on their boards, laughing with each other. Don't they know what happened here before? Doesn't the world mourn with me?

It wasn't meant to turn out like this. I was just trying to teach Teddy Stone a lesson. I knew he was going to be all right. I've never tried to kill anyone in my life. This is like a joke gone wrong. I would do anything to have Alex back. Already I feel so lonely without him.

Greeny wraps her arms around my waist and tries to comfort me. She doesn't understand. How can she?

Realizing that she will get nothing out of me, Greeny turns and wanders back to the café, leaving me alone. I look up and see that the surfers are talking excitedly to each other. One of them is diving underwater. I watch as he calls to his friend and dives again. The other one swims into shore with the boards, throwing them on to the sand. He turns to me.

'We've found a dead body,' he says, returning to the water.

My heart skips a beat. They bring him in, laying him on the sand. His head is cut, just above the ear, but the wound is not deep. He looks, for all the world, as if he is sleeping.

'Did you know him?' one of the surfers asks.

Saying nothing, Greeny leads them away, leaving me alone with Alex.

I crouch down beside him and look at his face. His eyes are closed. The troubled look has gone. He really seems to be having a wonderful sleep.

I remember him as he was this morning, in the Cave. I see him kneeling before me, his neck bared. And I see myself refusing, walking away.

Everything has changed since then. A thought . . . I smile briefly at the absurdity of it, then glance around the beach to make sure I am alone.

Can I do it? Can I *really* do it? Shouldn't I leave him, after all he has been through, to this peace? But how do I know he is at peace? He wanted to be with me. He said so. And I refused because he had other options. Now, what options does he have? But I can give him a way out. Then I won't be alone any more.

I lean over and lift the tangled hair away from his neck. I kneel down beside him, scooping up some water to wash the sand from his flesh.

As my lips brush the base of his neck, I taste the salt water . . .

His eyelids flicker. Soon he is looking up at me and I can see from his eyes that everything is going to be all right. He opens his mouth and seawater gushes out. There's a strand of seaweed caught between his teeth. It makes me want to laugh.

He tries to speak. He coughs and then I hear him try a sound. He breaks off to smile and I smile back. Then the words come.

'I think it's time we got out of this town.'

I don't need telling twice.

Dance with the Vampire

For my parents

CHAPTER I

MASSACHUSSETS, USA
1995

'STOP! ALEX, STOP!'
He was deaf to her words. There was nothing else for it. Ella darted forward and tugged him away. Alex resisted but finally released his grip. The boy fell back on to the grass, out of the pool of moonlight.

'You took too much! I've told you before. Only take as much as you need.'

'Yes. You told me!' He turned away, cloaking himself in darkness. When he faced her again, he looked ashamed.

Ella took his face in her hands. 'The change isn't easy. I know that. But you must remember that you're not a killer.'

'I never realized vampires were so full of scruples,' he said.

'Not all of us are.' She shivered. 'There are others who leave a trail of death and destruction behind them. But there's no need.'

Letting her hands fall from his face, she knelt down to examine the boy. He looked as though he was sleeping. The incision had been precise and he would certainly recover.

'It's time we were going,' Ella said.

They made their way, hand in hand, back through the woods to the road.

'Do you ever regret being this way?' she asked as they climbed inside the silver Thunderbird.

He shook his head. 'What about you? Are you sorry you made me a vampire, after all the trouble I've been to you?'

'You're no trouble.' She smiled at him, running her fingers through his hair. 'It takes time to learn these ways.' She hesitated before continuing. 'I was so lonely before you came into my life. All that matters to me now is that we're together.'

He leaned towards her and kissed her. 'Thank you,' he said, 'I needed to hear that.'

He started the engine and pushed his foot down hard on the throttle. The car revved into life and they were propelled along the highway, hurtling through the dark night.

Ella was in the shower when she heard the door open. She shut off the water and reached for a bathrobe. 'Alex, is that you?'

As she came out of the bathroom, she gasped.

'What do you think?' he asked, removing his sun-glasses. She looked up from his eyes to the top of his head. His hair had been cut to within a centimetre of his scalp.

'You look so different! Why?'

He shrugged. 'I needed a change. I thought you'd like it.' He set a paper bag down on the table. 'I bought coffee and doughnuts. Here, have one.'

She took the doughnut and removed the lid from the cup of coffee, watching the steam spiral to the ceiling.

It was a routine start to the day – waking in another motel someplace new, finding breakfast. Ella had lost count of the towns they had passed through. They had probably driven more miles in the Thunderbird in the past month than its previous owner had in years.

She glanced down at her bag. Souvenirs of their times in the States poured out on to the floor – postcards, coasters and snapshots. These flimsy bits of paper filled her with happiness, reminding her of conversations they'd had, places they'd been, things they had seen for the first time together.

'Ella, can we talk?'

She glanced up, snapping out of her daydream. Alex looked serious, tense. She had not seen that expression for a while. 'What's wrong?'

'It's time I went back,' he said. 'Charlie needs me. I have to go back to Oakport.'

'OK. Of course, I understand.' She was ashamed of the feelings of disappointment and jealousy. It wasn't right to feel jealous of Alex's family or to wish that, like her, he was all alone in the world. As they had travelled around during the past month, he had acted as if he had no cares and she had let herself believe it was true. Now, she had to accept that he had hidden his true feelings. Alex still had a brother and it was inevitable that he would want to return to him.

'Do you feel ready?'

'I'm as ready now as I'll ever be. Besides, the longer I leave it, the worse it'll be . . . for Charlie.'

'Have you thought about what you'll tell your aunt and uncle?'

He shook his head. 'Not really. I mean . . . obviously, I can't tell them the truth . . . the *whole* truth. Maybe you can help me come up with a convincing story.'

'Are you saying I'm a good liar?' She smiled at him playfully. But he wasn't in the mood for jokes. She adopted a more serious tone. 'Are you sure this really is the best thing . . . for Charlie and for you?'

'I can't leave him there.' Alex's voice was raw emotion. 'He's nine years old. He's my brother. I can't leave him with that man . . . the man who murdered our parents. Charlie can't protect himself. He needs me.'

What more could she ask? How else could she try to dissuade him? Now it was up to her. Should she go with him or end it here and now? For how could she tell Alex that, concerned as she was for him, an entirely different fear possessed her. A voice in her head – a voice long dormant – was warning her not to go to Oakport.

PRAGUE, 1782

PRINCESS ELISABETH TOOK a deep breath as she entered the ballroom. Her father – the emperor – had forbidden her presence at the ball. He thought her too young at fourteen to attend such an occasion. But there was no way she could stay away. It was her last chance to declare her love for Count Eduard de Savigny, before he left the court.

Thankfully, her older sister Anna had come up with a plan.

'Don't despair, Lissie – you shall borrow one of my dresses! And we'll all be wearing masks. You'll go in first – they'll all think it's me. I'll come along later once everyone's too involved in the party to notice.'

And so, here she was, entering the ballroom. She could hardly contain her delight as the waves of party-goers stepped back to bow and curtsy to her. She heard someone remark how graceful the Princess Anna seemed tonight. Little did they know it was really little Lissie in disguise!

The ballroom looked enchanting with flickering candles at every turn – some real, others reflections in the mirrors that lined the walls. Elisabeth glanced up above to the painted clouds that seemed to float across the ceiling. The cherubs sitting upon them looked as if they might shoot real arrows down into the crowd.

Elisabeth smiled to herself. The arrow of love had already pierced her heart. Since his arrival at court a month before, Count Eduard de Savigny had dominated her waking thoughts and, later, her dreams. But it was an impossible love. Tomorrow he would leave for Vienna to continue his experiments in alchemy. He would take with him both the gold and good wishes of the emperor himself. And, with them, the heart of a princess.

How many times had she watched him from afar at the dinner table? He was the most handsome man she had ever seen – his hair like long strands of gold, his eyes greener than the emeralds she wore around her neck. He was quite perfect.

And now she longed to find him in the crowd. But just as a mask hid her identity, so the masks around her made it impossible to tell who was who.

She was led on to the dance floor by a man who revealed himself to be a baron. He seemed keener to tell her about his livestock than to know anything about her. She could not have been more delighted when the music ended and she was released into the crowd. She wandered around, continuing to speculate which mask covered the face of her beloved.

'Have you found him?'

'Anna, is that you?'

'Of course!'

She hugged her sister but shook her head. 'No, I haven't found him yet. I've been too busy trying to solve Baron Kempinski's farming difficulties!'

Princess Anna laughed. 'He's such a bore. I believe he thinks the mere mention of his estate will melt a lady's heart. But now, let us see. Where can your count be?'

'May I have this dance?' The stranger's voice caught both sisters by surprise. Elisabeth waited for Anna to disappear with her suitor to the dance floor, but then she realized that the man was reaching out for her own hand.

Surprised, she returned to the dance floor. The man spoke little as they danced – a relief after the talkative baron. Elisabeth lost herself in the waltz music. As the music ended, she curtsied and began to walk away.

'Wait! Please . . . dance with me once again.' Flattered, she turned around. This time, as they performed the intricate steps, she noticed that he was watching her closely. She flushed with unexpected pleasure. They danced again and again. He was a fine dancer.

'Look, it's snowing!'

There was much excitement as the doors were opened and several couples ran out through them into the night air.

'Let's go outside.'

He took her hand and led her out through the door. They walked in silence towards the castle ramparts and gazed down over the city while eddies of snowflakes showered them from above.

'Take off your mask.'

His words filled her with fear.

'Please, I want to see your face. To see if you are as beautiful as I imagine.'

No man had ever spoken to her that way before. In spite of the cold night air, she felt her heart melting inside her. Suddenly, she wanted nothing more than to see the face of her mysterious suitor.

'I shall indeed remove my mask, but you must take off yours too. Yes? And I have one further condition – our identities must only be known to one another.'

'If that is your desire.'

He reached behind his head to unfasten his mask. She did the same. Her mask fell away.

'Princess Elisabeth!'

'You must not tell my father!'

But as his mask fell, all her fears receded. She found herself looking into the face of Count Eduard de Savigny. He smiled and lowered his head to kiss her. Could this really be happening? Maybe her love had finally led her into madness.

But no, he spoke. He asked her to walk with him. And so they left the castle and the music behind them, walking on towards the bridge. Towards the white, deserted city.

As they reached the bridge, he stopped and drew her towards him. He planted the sweetest of kisses on her lips and cheeks, beneath her ears and down the curve of her neck.

Elisabeth stroked his golden hair, looking up to the eddies of snowflakes. Suddenly, she felt a searing pain as if twin blades had punctured the base of her neck. And yet, as the pain gave way to numbness, she was powerless to do anything but watch the falling snow.

'What have you done? What have you done to me?'

He did not answer, but merely raised his bloodstained mouth in a strange smile.

CHAPTER II

OAKPORT, MAINE

THEY ARRIVED IN Oakport just after nightfall. The town was quiet. As they drove along the edge of the ocean, Ella could make out the dark surface of the churning water. Suddenly a beam from the lighthouse swept over the waves. Then the light was gone and the dark returned.

'Is it far to Shadow Street?' Ella asked.

'Let's not go there tonight,' Alex said. Ella was surprised but relieved. 'We're both tired,' Alex continued. 'Let's get some sleep and head over there tomorrow.'

'Where are we going to sleep?' Ella asked.

'The boathouse,' Alex said. 'We'll sleep at the boathouse.'

He turned the Thunderbird away from the main road on to a narrower track. There were fewer and fewer houses along this way. Pretty soon there was scarcely any sign of habitation at all and they were driving through a corridor of thick black spruces.

Ella felt a sudden chill. She was tired and

hungry. And she somehow still feared what awaited them here in Oakport.

At last, the forest thinned out and they were heading towards water again. This time it wasn't the ocean but a lake. The placid waters contrasted strongly with the churning surf she had glimpsed before.

Alex brought the car to a standstill beside a wooden boathouse nestling at the edge of the lake. He switched off the ignition. Ella wished they could have continued driving. As long as they were moving, they were free.

There was a padlock on the door. Alex crouched down on the ground, searching among the stones. He pulled out a key and opened the door.

He took a book of matches from his pocket and struck a match. The tiny light sparked and died all too quickly. He struck another match, shielding it from the draught. This led him to the hurricane lamp. A third match lit the lamp. There was still oil inside it and the lamp filled with light, illuminating the room. 'I'll get our bags,' he said.

Ella was left alone in the room. There were dust sheets on the chairs. She lifted one. It floated away like a ghost. She removed the other sheets and piled them in a corner.

Alex had told her all about his family and the happy weekends they had spent here. The evidence of those times was everywhere. On the shelves, scores of old paperbacks nestled by battered boxes of Monopoly and Twister. There were maps and other guides to the woods, and framed family photographs. As she took in all the Culler family's possessions, she heard Alex's voice retelling his story.

We were a close family. Before Ethan Sawyer came into our lives. Before even Aunt Sarah moved back from the West Coast. It was just Mom and Dad and Charlie and me, then. Just a regular family doing all the regular things. Most weekends, we'd go trekking in the woods. We often stayed at the boathouse. It was my grandfather's. It was like a second home to me.

We didn't have the boat then – not a proper one. It was Ethan who got us into all that. Before him, we just had a small rowing boat. Sometimes I'd take Charlie out in it and we'd fool around on the lake. Mom was always worried about him.

When Sarah came back east, everything changed. She came along with us on a camping trip. After that, she was with us every weekend. And then she met Ethan and he came along too. I guess we enjoyed having them around. Mom certainly liked Sarah's company.

It all happened so fast. One minute, we were getting to know Sarah all over again. The next, Ethan Sawyer rolled right into our lives. And just as we were starting to make sense of it all, they went missing for a weekend. Turned out they'd flown to Vegas and got married.

It was the same when Ethan bought the boat. He just drove us out to the harbour and it was waiting for us. After that, we spent our weekends on the ocean. Dad had always been interested in sailing and Ethan said that he should treat the boat as his own – that we all should. He said it was his gift to us for letting him into our family . . .

She could see them now – like a snapshot come to life: Charlie sitting on the rug, playing cards with Alex; their dad and Ethan poring over a chart, plotting out the sailing trip, and their mother and Sarah sorting out food supplies in the kitchen.

The picture faded as Alex brought their bags into the room and closed the door behind him. 'We'll stay here tonight. I'll see if there's any food left in the kitchen.' Ella was unnerved by Alex's composure. It was as if nothing terrible had happened – as if his mother and father had never died – and his only worry was what to cook for supper.

She followed him into the kitchen to find him already pulling cans of food from the larder. 'It's not gourmet but we'll make do,' he said. 'I'm starving. Are you ready to eat now?' She nodded, although she had no appetite, and he began opening up the cans.

She left him in the kitchen and returned to the living room. Again, she imagined the Cullers as they had once been and how they might have welcomed her among them, excited to meet Alex's new girlfriend.

'Why don't you go out on to the deck?' Alex called from the kitchen. 'There's a fantastic view of the lake.'

On one side of the room, there were double doors leading out on to the deck. Ella opened them and stepped out into the cool evening air. The lake was a dark indigo now. A small rowing boat was moored to the deck. Ella watched it bob on the inky water. Alex's words flooded back to her.

We should never have gone out that day. The coastguard forecast a storm late in the after-noon. Ethan said we'd have plenty of time to go out and return by then – we'd been planning the trip for weeks, we couldn't waste the chance now. And so, we set off. Mom and Dad and Charlie and Ethan and me. Sarah stayed at home – she was helping out with some bake sale or something . . .

At first it seemed like great sailing weather. There was just enough of a breeze and the sun was strong. As soon as we left the harbour it began to get rougher. Out past the headland, Mom wanted to turn back – she was worried that Charlie would get sea-sick. Ethan said that

*we could ride it out – that Charlie was a natural
sailor. Of course, Charlie agreed. Dad told Mom
not to worry – that Ethan knew what he was
doing.*

*The storm hit suddenly – earlier than forecast.
Ethan tried to turn the boat around, but the gale
was too strong for him. Dad and I tried to help
but we were thrown back and forth across the
boat. I remember Mom trying to keep hold of
Charlie. The boat was bouncing on the water
and we were all clinging on for our lives.*

*The next thing I knew, I was in the water and
the boat was on top of me. Everything seemed to
happen in slow motion then. I could see our stuff
sinking down to the ocean floor. Somehow, my
life jacket had come loose and I realized I'd have
to swim my way back up. When I surfaced, the
boat was a wreck. I couldn't see any of the
others.*

*Then Ethan and Charlie went past in the
dinghy that we kept at the back of the boat.
Charlie looked unconscious. Ethan was rowing
him ashore. I thought he was going to come
back for me. I swam around, trying to keep
calm, searching for my mom and dad. I called
out to them but they didn't answer. I guess I lost
track of time.*

*It was like a dream – a nightmare. The sea
water was icy cold and I was getting more and
more confused. I wasn't sure I could keep tread-
ing water much longer.*

Then, something snapped inside me. I knew that if I didn't start swimming, I would never make it ashore. In spite of my numbness, my arms and legs took over, propelling me towards the land. And I left my parents to die . . .

'Supper's ready.' Ella shuddered as his voice, his hand on her shoulder, brought her back from her imaginings.

'Are you all right?' he asked. 'You look very pale.'

She found it difficult to understand how he could be so calm. 'Doesn't it disturb you being back here?'

He shook his head. 'Not really. We had so many great times here. I feel I'm close to my family again. I know it's weird but I feel like they're here with us.'

Later, after they had washed up the dinner things and closed up the house for the night, Alex took the hurricane lamp and led the way upstairs.

'Wait!' Ella said, her eyes settling on one of the photographs. It was half-hidden behind several others and veiled in dust. As Alex brought the light back towards her, Ella brushed the surface of the glass clean. She looked down at the picture. 'That's him, isn't it?'

Alex nodded. 'That's him – the man who murdered my parents.'

In the picture, Ethan Sawyer was sitting in a

dinghy, between Alex and Charlie. One of Ethan's hands was resting on Charlie's shoulder, the other waving at the photographer. All three of them were smiling.

He had thick, pale blond hair and deep blue eyes and looked younger than his thirty-five years. He was strikingly handsome – not at all what she'd expected from the picture Alex had painted.

She found herself drawn back to his eyes, which seemed to come right out of the photograph, as if he was talking to her. She rested the picture back down on the shelf beside the others.

But later, out of the depths of sleep, Ethan Sawyer's face returned to her. She found herself transfixed by his gaze. This time, he was holding out his hand to her.

She sat bolt upright with the shock, as if she had dived into freezing water. Now she realized how right she had been to fear their arrival in Oakport.

PRAGUE, 1782

'COME HERE,' HE said. With one hand, he held back the branches and with the other reached out to help steady her balance on the rough ground.

She took his hand gratefully and he drew her close beside him.

'Now look.'

She stared through the gap he had made through the branches, into the glade. A boy was standing there. She turned to Eduard, confused. 'What's he doing here in the forest?'

'Not so loud!' he whispered in reply. 'He might hear us.'

It was then that she noticed a peculiar light emanating from Eduard's eyes. Simultaneously, her own heart began to thud. She looked back at the boy. Her initial feelings had been concern for his safety. But now her anxiety about him wore off, replaced by an altogether different sensation.

'Don't fight it,' Eduard whispered in her ear, as if he had read her mind. 'Let the hunger flow through you.'

His words had the power of command over her. She felt her body give itself over to this feeling – shockingly alien but at the same time perfectly natural.

The rest happened in a blur of speed. Before she knew it, she was inside the glade itself. Eduard had the boy in his arms and had punctured his frail neck. She watched, fascinated.

Her body was on fire. Eduard looked up at her, his eyes brimming with light. She could not wait any longer.

She crouched down beside him. She saw the puncture marks already beginning to close. No. That mustn't happen. Not before she too had her fill. Without further delay, she dug her teeth down into his neck and waited.

Nothing happened. She felt a burning sense of dissatisfaction – a fear that her hunger would be unfulfilled. And then it came. The rich blood seemed to explode like fireworks on her tongue. It raced into her mouth and down . . .

She could not stop, would not stop. Only by taking more could she sate her needs. And yet, as she drank, the need seemed only to grow stronger, deeper. She feasted until at last she was overcome by exhaustion and fell back on to the ground.

When she came to, she did not recognize her surroundings. She was still in the forest but not in the glade. She looked around curiously, noticing the reflection of the moon on the water. She was at the side of a small lake.

'I brought you here to clean yourself,' Eduard said.

To clean herself. What did he mean? She pulled herself to her knees and looked down into the water. She drew back, terrified. She had seen a devil lurking beneath the water's surface.

Then her heart began to pound. Slowly, she looked down again and saw her own face. It was dirty with blood.

Her thoughts turned to the boy. Now the hunger was gone and her thoughts were once again for his safety. She gazed up at Eduard. 'Where is he? We have to get back to him . . . to help him.'

Eduard shook his head. 'It's too late.'

'No!' She opened her mouth to scream but the word emerged as a hoarse whisper. She looked down once again at her own reflection. 'What have I done? What kind of monster am I?'

CHAPTER III

AS SHE DRESSED the following morning, Ella found herself shaking. The voice deep within her was telling her to turn and run but she couldn't leave Alex to face this alone – especially if what she feared was true. Whatever the danger to herself, she had to stay with him.

Alex was tense. He didn't speak during breakfast, except to check this or that detail of his story. Finally, he glanced at his watch. 'Shall we go?'

By daylight the lake looked quite different, thought Ella, glancing behind to the water as they drove back into the forest. For the first time, she was able to see across to the other side of the lake. Alex's voice returned to her.

I came to late in the night. At first, I couldn't remember what had happened. Then it hit me – the churning waves, all the pain, all the loss. In the darkness, I couldn't tell where I was. Then I must have lost consciousness again. When I next woke, it was morning. I was tired and hungry.

When I finally found the nearest town, I realized I was way up the coast. We'd driven through the place once or twice. There was a gas station. I went into the washrooms. I could see in the mirror that I was a mess. There was a deep wound just below my neck. I cleaned myself up as best I could and hitched a ride back towards Oakport.

When I got back to town, I saw the newspaper. The lead story was about the accident. It reported that three bodies had been found. My dad's, my mom's and a third. It was more beaten up than the others but presumed to be mine. As far as they were concerned, I was dead.

Ethan was quoted saying all kinds of things. That he'd taken the dinghy around and around trying to find us and only then gone back to shore. That he'd broken down when he recognized my sweater on the body. He was lying. And that made me think. What if this wasn't an accident after all? What if he wanted us to die? All of us, except Charlie?

As they neared the peak of the cliff, the church came into view, swimming in a sea of graves. 'This is the place, isn't it?' Ella asked. Alex nodded, bringing the car to a standstill.

They walked through the gateway and round past the church. Ella felt she had been here before. She seemed even to know where the graves were. She crouched down to read the inscriptions.

Adam Culler, 1952–1995. Beloved husband of Charlotte and father of Alexander and Charles . . .

Charlotte Baines Culler, 1954–1995 . . .

She turned to the last grave, knowing what to expect. Still the words chilled her.

Alexander Culler, 1978–1995. Son of Adam and Charlotte. 'In their death they were not divided' . . .

'Look! Someone brought me flowers,' said Alex, leaning across her to pick up a bunch of tattered roses. The petals fell from the stems and were carried away on the breeze. Ella watched them until the specks of colour disappeared from view, swallowed by the blackness of the spruces at the cliff-edge.

I watched the funeral from the edge of the churchyard. I was cold and tired and my wound throbbed. I wanted to run to Charlie – to show him I was still alive. But I knew I couldn't trust Ethan Sawyer.

Neither Ella nor Alex heard the car door close. The sound was drowned out by the noise of the wind in the trees. The voices too were muffled by the breeze. It was only as Ella turned that she saw the couple closing the gate and walking out towards the graves. Alex had seen them too. He looked suddenly panic-stricken.

'What is it? What's wrong?' Ella asked.

'Quick! Get down!' Alex pulled Ella back to the ground. He looked frantically from left to right.

'Over here!' He began crawling towards a pair of large headstones, a few rows back. Ella followed, her hands and knees scraping the wet grass. As she started to understand what was happening, her heart began to pound. They reached the cover of the stones just as the couple came to a stop a few rows away.

'It's a good thing I brought fresh roses.' The woman's voice was close now, clear. Ella thought she could hear the flowers being removed from their wrapping.

'I'll take that, shall I?' This time it was the man. Ella could tell from the sounds that followed that they were arranging the flowers on the graves.

'They won't last long in this wind,' said the man.

'That doesn't matter. I just want them to know we're thinking about them. That we still . . .' She broke off, overcome by tears.

The man spoke softly. 'Not an hour goes by when I don't think about that day. If only I had been quicker, had done more. If only I had saved them . . .'

Ella glanced at Alex. His dark expression confirmed her suspicions. The man and woman were Ethan and Sarah Sawyer – Alex's uncle and aunt.

'You couldn't have done anything more,' Sarah said – the words pushing through the tears. 'At least you saved Charlie. And I'm sure they're all grateful for that.'

'I just wish . . . I just wish I could have saved . . . if not Adam and Charlotte then at least Alex. He was only seventeen. That's no age . . .'

Ella turned to Alex again. He was frowning. Perhaps he too was confused. It certainly didn't sound like Ethan had wanted him to die.

'I'd give anything to have him back,' Ethan said.

Ella saw the effect of the words on Alex. It was as if he had been put into a trance. He stood up slowly, deliberately, until he reached his full height, and stared, unblinking, at Ethan.

Ella heard Sarah let out a wail. Ella raised her eyes above the gravestone and saw Ethan Sawyer in the flesh for the first time.

His long, golden hair was like a flame in the dark churchyard. His eyes were fixed on Alex. 'It's a miracle!' Ethan said, approaching Alex and hugging him. Tears streamed from his eyes. Alex remained inanimate.

Sarah too moved towards Alex. Ethan stepped back, making room for her, smiling through his tears.

'Is it really you?' Sarah's voice was weak. She held out her hand, the tips of her fingers making contact with Alex's face. Hesitantly, she traced the outline of his jaw. 'Welcome back,' she said, hugging him. 'Welcome back.'

For the first time, Alex's face gave way to emotion. Ella saw him hug Sarah back. They remained in each other's arms as the wind swept around them. Ella watched them, sensing that Ethan's eyes were fixed on her. She willed herself not to look at him. She was not yet ready for this. Would she ever be?

At last, Ethan rested his hand on Sarah's shoulder. 'Let's take Alex home.' Sarah reluctantly drew back but one hand still clutched Alex tightly.

'Come on,' she said. 'I'll take you to the car.'

Ella felt suddenly exposed and abandoned. She knew that Ethan Sawyer was watching her but she still jumped when he spoke.

'I'm not accustomed to meeting people in churchyards.'

It was him. Of course it was him. He looked a little different in this incarnation but there was not a trace of doubt in her mind.

'I'm Ethan Sawyer,' he said, offering his hand. Why was he pretending? They both knew who he was.

She did not take his hand. She looked away. Alex and Sarah had almost reached the church gate. She began to run after them but her movements were sluggish. In a moment, he was at her side. He looked at her, sadly.

'Why do you always run from me, Elisabeth?' he asked.

She stared up into his eyes. At once, she felt the familiar dizziness. She lost all sense of where she was, feeling herself pulled backwards into a tunnel through time. All around her, old scenes replayed from their times together. Now she was walking across the African plains. Now, wandering through the gardens of an Italian villa. Now, ordering drinks in a French café. And always with him. Over two hundred years and still it seemed she could never leave him. Further and further back through the centuries she journeyed, until once again she heard the waltz music and looked down to find herself in the green ball gown.

CHAPTER IV

'COME ON INSIDE,' Sarah said, unlocking the door. 'I'll make us some coffee.'

While Sarah busied herself in the kitchen, the others waited in the living room. It was spacious and simply furnished. On the walls were stunning black and white photographs. They were all nature studies – grasses wet with dew, moss-covered bark and driftwood in the surf. Ella read the signature in the corner of each frame – *Ethan Sawyer*.

'They're wonderful, aren't they?' Sarah said, bringing out a tray of mugs. 'You should see Ethan's new exhibition. It's spectacular.'

'Where's Charlie?' Alex asked abruptly. Sarah immediately fell silent.

'He's at school, Alex,' Ethan said calmly. 'Where else?' He poured a mug of coffee and handed it to Ella.

She took the mug, turning away from his eyes. 'Don't fight it.'

He hadn't spoken but the words were clear inside her head. Ella began to shake. She couldn't control it. The hot coffee began to seep over the sides of the mug, spattering over Ella's jeans and down on to the floor. Finally, the mug itself slipped from her grasp and dropped on to the rug.

'I'm so sorry.' Ella rushed towards the kitchen, but Sarah had already grabbed a damp cloth.

'It's nothing,' Sarah said, mopping up the liquid. 'We're all shaken up. After everything that's happened today, how could we not be? Here, give me the mug. I'll fill it up for you.'

Sarah handed a fresh mug to Ella and went to sit beside Alex on the sofa. Ella's hand was steadier now. She had to pull herself together – for Alex's sake.

'So, Alex,' Ethan said, 'where do we begin?'

Alex took a deep breath as he began the story he'd so carefully rehearsed. 'I was found up the coast by fishermen, near Archangel Point. They took me to the hospital. It was three days before I regained consciousness. By then, my wounds were starting to heal. I stayed at the hospital a full month . . .'

'Which hospital?' Sarah asked.

'The one up near Archangel Point . . .' Ella saw that Alex was looking nervous.

'I don't remember there being a hospital up there.' Sarah looked to Ethan, but he did not respond.

'It's only a small hospital,' Alex said.

'Why didn't they contact us?' Sarah said.

Alex looked down at the palms of his hands. 'I told them not to.'

'You did?' Sarah looked hurt.

'I wanted to make sure I was fully recovered before I came back for . . . to Charlie.'

Ethan nodded.

'I don't understand.' Sarah seemed torn between tears of anger and rage. 'It's as if you *wanted* us to think you were dead.'

Ella studied Sarah's face. It was a strange face for a woman in her mid-thirties, at once innocent as a child's yet etched with worry-lines. Alex had told Ella that Sarah had gone through a bad time before she met Ethan. Ella wondered what Sarah's life was like now. How much did she know about Ethan? And how did Ethan treat her?

'Where are you staying now?' Ethan asked.

'Out at the boathouse.'

'How did you two meet?' Sarah turned suddenly to Ella.

'At the hospital.' Ella shifted in her chair as she relayed her part of their elaborate lie. 'I was visiting my cousin. She was in a road accident. She was in the next bed to Alex. We got talking and soon became . . . friends.'

'But you're not from here.' Sarah took a sip of coffee. 'Your accent . . .'

'I'm English, but I have an aunt and uncle out here. I've been staying with them for the summer.'

'Do they live around here? Maybe we know them?'

Ethan laughed. 'We don't know absolutely

everyone in Maine, hon. I think that's enough questions for now, don't you?'

'Of course.' Sarah nodded, hugging Alex.

'When will Charlie be home?' Alex asked.

'Oh, not for another few hours,' Ethan said, looking at his watch. 'He has a violin lesson after school. You remember, Alex, how important his music is to him.'

'I can't wait to meet him,' Ella told Sarah. 'Alex has told me so much about him.'

Ethan looked from Ella to Sarah to Alex. 'I think it's best if we talk to Charlie first; prepare him. I'm still reeling from seeing you again. Imagine what it will be like for him.'

Alex frowned. 'I want to see him . . . as soon as possible.'

'Of course,' Ethan nodded. 'We'll talk to him when he gets home.'

'I want to see him,' Alex repeated, standing up. 'I want him to know that I'm . . .' He caught Ella's eye. 'That I'm . . . back.'

Ethan also turned to Ella. 'I'm sure *you* agree, Ella. It's better not to rush things.'

Unnerved, she walked over to Alex and took his hand.

'Go back to the boathouse,' Ethan said. 'We'll speak to Charlie and tell him you'll come over tomorrow.'

'Maybe they'd be more comfortable at a motel?' Sarah said. 'If it's a question of money . . .'

'No,' Alex interrupted. 'We'll be fine.'

They walked out into the hallway. Alex turned to leave but Sarah wouldn't let him go before she had hugged him again.

Ethan held out his hand to Ella. She took it, nervous of making physical contact with him.

'It was good to meet you,' he said. 'And I want to thank you.'

'What for?' Ella asked, surprised.

'For bringing Alex back,' Ethan said.

Although his tone remained even, his grip tightened around her hand, not letting her move until he released her, silently reminding her how powerful he was. She trembled. If there was one thing she had learned over the years, it was not to cross this man. Yet that was what she had done by bringing Alex back. And he was only too aware of it.

PRAGUE, 1782

PRINCESS ELISABETH OFTEN dreamed of her family and of the life she had left behind. More than anything, she wanted to go back. But with the passing of each day, the possibility of escape seemed ever more remote.

Living in the forest, she felt no different to the wild beasts who roamed its pathways. By day, she wandered around – trying to come to terms with her own savagery. But by night she stalked her prey with an eager anticipation and, increasingly, deadly precision.

Eduard seemed pleased with her company. Thinking of the dashing figure he had cut at court, she was constantly amazed to see him live this way – stalking this wilderness like a jungle cat. Yet in spite of the strangeness of this world and the transformation they had both undergone, she was still drawn to him – in many ways, more strongly now than ever.

But he told her that they would soon leave the forest. He was making plans to return to his castle in a neighbouring province. Elisabeth felt a flush of excitement at the idea of once again living within walls and sleeping on a plump. mattress rather than the rough forest floor. But leaving the forest meant leaving Prague far behind and closing for ever the door to her past life. Eduard had told her before that she could never go back.

'Absolutely not. I forbid it.'

'But I only want to say goodbye.'

He laughed coldly. 'They won't even let you through the castle gates looking the way you do now.'

It was true, she supposed.

'At least let me see the castle one last time.'

He shook his head. 'It's for your own good. We'll talk no more of this. I have to make plans . . .'

His arrogance was beyond all bounds. If he did not want something to be, he simply shut all possibility of it out of his mind. But in her own head, the thought of returning home did not fade so easily. As Eduard busied himself with 'plans', she roamed through the lonely forest, picturing herself back within the labyrinthian castle chambers.

She reached out for the trunk of a tree, imagining it to be one of the columns in the castle ballroom. She made believe that the bird song was orchestra music and that, once again, she was on her way to the dance. She was still wearing her ball dress, she reminded herself, even if it was in tatters now and blackened by spatters of mud and blood.

The daydream would not go away. She knew

that, whatever Eduard said, she had to go back. She was sure she would be all right if only she could make it as far as the gates. She knew the guards by name. They had always had a soft spot for the emperor's daughters. One of them would be sure to recognize her and let her back inside.

And so, she too began to make plans – noting, by the shifting patterns of light, the times when Eduard left her alone. Exploring the furthest reaches of the forest, she determined the quickest route out. And one morning as Eduard left her, casually remarking that he would be gone a matter of hours, she set off.

She had found that, among the changes in her physical being, she could move much faster than before. She felt exhilarated by her speed and this new mastery over her body, convinced that she was heading towards her salvation.

As she hurried through the rain-slick streets, she became increasingly aware of her ragged appearance. Dusk was falling and she was glad that the deepening shadows hid her shame.

At last, she crossed the bridge just beneath the castle. Her heart beat faster and faster as she began the climb to the castle gates.

The guard ignored her at first, thinking that she had only come to beg. When she called him by his name, he stopped dead in his tracks and a strange look passed over his face.

'I can't explain now, Lajos,' she gasped, 'but

just let me inside so I can see my father. I'll see you're rewarded.'

'Princess Elisabeth!' he rasped, a rebel tear sliding over his rough skin. 'Just knowing you're safe is all the reward I need.'

He opened the gate and she stumbled inside, tears of relief flooding down her dirty cheeks. As the gate closed behind her, she glanced back, and her heart suddenly lurched within her. Eduard was there on the other side of the gate, fixing her with furious eyes.

She froze, terrified. His mouth was closed and yet she heard his voice clear and loud inside her head. 'You can never escape from me. You can never run away from what you've become.'

'You're shivering.' The old guard turned her back towards the castle. 'We must get you inside into the warmth.'

CHAPTER V

'HE'S TRYING TO stop me seeing Charlie.'

Ella watched Alex pace the length of the living room once again. He'd been this way all afternoon – ever since they'd arrived back at the boathouse.

'No,' she said calmly, 'he just wasn't there.'

'Maybe we should have waited.'

Ella touched him gently on the arm, stopping him in his tracks. 'You can't keep torturing yourself like this. You'll see him tomorrow.'

'I know.' Alex shrugged as she slipped her arms around his waist. 'It's just I've come so far . . . waited so long for this. I just wish I knew everything was going to be OK.'

'Everything's going to be fine.' She kissed him. 'Why don't we go for a drive?'

'Where to?'

'Since when did we need anywhere special to go? Let's just get in the car.'

They drove along the cliff road, watching the sun sink down into the dark ocean. Alex seemed to lose himself in the action of driving, his hands and mind fixed on the wheel. Ella felt the cool breeze running through her hair. She shivered. She could not get Ethan Sawyer out of her mind.

After a while, the cliff road turned inland and they found themselves driving through a more built-up area. Ella watched Alex as he manoeuvred the Thunderbird through the streets. His face was marked with grim determination. She wondered if he was lost but something stopped her from asking.

She turned to look at the houses to one side of the street. The street lamps illuminated broad gardens sweeping down to the road. Alex slowed the car and Ella caught a good look at a house where a party was going on. One of her favourite songs was playing and inside the building people were dancing.

At first she did not realize that the car had stopped. She was transfixed by the view into the house. A tall, blonde-haired girl was dancing in the centre of the room. She was a great dancer, pretty too. A couple of guys tried to get her attention. She danced with one for a moment or two, but soon turned away. When the other approached her, she smiled and did just the same. Ella liked her style.

As the song ended and the girl moved out of view Ella glanced at Alex. His eyes were still fixed on the lighted window. Ella realized in a moment that it was no fluke that they had ended up in this street, outside this very house.

She hesitated before speaking. 'Do you want to go inside?'

Alex smiled softly. 'Are you suggesting we crash the party?'

'I get the impression you know the people inside.'

Her heart beat fast as he turned towards her and met her eyes. He seemed surprised but relieved. 'Yes,' he said, 'I know her . . . at least I did.'

A car roared up beside them. They both turned as the driver manoeuvred it wildly into a space on the other side of the street. A young couple got out from the car. They were obviously on their way to the party. The girl began walking towards the front door, but the guy caught her, drawing her into a kiss. As she pulled away, she looked straight at Alex and Ella. Her face paled and her eyes narrowed in on Alex.

Alex too seemed shaken. But in a moment he managed to collect his senses and switch the engine on again. He steered the Thunderbird back into the centre of the street. As they drove away, Ella glanced back at the girl. She was waving her hand towards the car and crying out words Ella could not hear. Her boyfriend held her back. Then, Ella lost sight of them as Alex turned the car out of the street.

They raced back towards the lake. Before the road broke off towards the boathouse, Ella nudged Alex.

'Stop the car.'

'What?'

'You heard me. Pull over. Just here . . . by the lake.'

He followed her instructions, bringing the car to a standstill at the water's edge.

'Now, get out of the car . . . No! Don't turn off the ignition, just get out.'

He was confused but did as she said. She leaned over and flicked on the radio, twisting the dial until she found a rock and roll station. She turned the volume up.

'Let's dance,' she said, walking towards him and reaching for his hand.

His movements were awkward at first. Perhaps he felt self-conscious too. But he soon started to loosen up.

After a couple of up-tempo songs, the DJ slowed it down. Ella and Alex danced close together, their movements becoming ever slower and more slight. Then, he pulled her closer still and their mouths met.

Afterwards, she took his hand and they sat down on the bonnet of the car.

'Do you want to talk about it?' she asked.

'I don't know what to say,' he said.

'I've been there,' she said. 'I know what it's like. On the outside, looking in.'

He nodded.

'You feel like the world you used to be part of is out of your reach. Like the people you once

133

knew are trapped on one side of the window and you're on the other – all alone.'

'Yes. But I'm not alone.' He lifted her mouth towards his and kissed her again.

As he drew away again, she asked the question that would not go away. 'The girl – the blonde that was dancing – she was more than just a friend, wasn't she?'

'Her name is Carrie . . . Carrie Jordan. We went out for a while.' He looked sad. Ella felt that, in spite of all he had said, he would do anything to have his old life back again.

'Did you love her?' Why was she doing this to herself – asking the very questions that threatened to hurt her most?

'I guess I did . . . in a way.'

He saw that she was upset. He reached for her hands and looked deep into her eyes. 'It was all very innocent. We went to the movies and parties and . . . we had fun together. But it was kids' stuff compared to the way I feel about you. I want to be with you always. Whatever happens now, it's you and me.'

She slipped her hands free and reached up to his shoulders. They kissed with more intensity than ever before.

'How about you?' he asked her as they parted. 'Have you been in love before?'

His question took her by surprise. 'Come on,' he persisted, 'tell me or I'll tickle you!'

She was not in the mood for jokes. She

shrugged off his hands and turned away, looking down into the deep, inky waters of the lake.

'I'm sorry, Ella. I was only fooling around. You don't have to tell me . . . if you don't want to.'

'No.' She turned back towards him. 'No. I do want to.'

'Then what's wrong?'

'It's a long story. I first met him a long time ago.'

'How long?'

'Two hundred years ago.'

'What was his name?'

'He called himself Eduard de Savigny *then* . . .'

'Very grand!' She was aware that it must all seem like a fairy tale to him.

'He was a count,' Ella continued. 'But then I was a princess.'

Alex was clearly intrigued. 'What do you mean that he called himself de Savigny *then*?'

She paused before continuing. 'He was a vampire, Alex. He was the one who made *me* a vampire. He was called de Savigny then, but he has had many other names since . . . as have I.'

'I don't understand.'

'It's called "blood possession". I only became Ella Ryder a couple of years ago. I drained Ella of her blood and my . . . "spirit" – I guess that's what you'd call it – transferred into her body.'

'So what would happen if you were to drain someone else's blood?'

'Then, providing I got it right, my spirit would enter that person's body.'

'And what would happen to the original Ella?'

'It depends,' she said, carefully. 'Things can go wrong. It's not something we do for fun. But every now and then, there is a reason to assume a new identity.'

'So this de Savigny, he's still out there . . . in a different body?'

She nodded.

'Imagine.' Alex's mind was working overtime. 'Imagine if you were to meet him . . . oh, no, of course, if he was in a different body, you wouldn't recognize him.'

She was about to correct him, to tell him that it didn't matter what you looked like on the surface – you could still recognize one another. But she couldn't go on.

'I wonder where he is now,' Alex said, unable to let it go. 'I wonder who he is.'

CHAPTER VI

ETHAN OPENED THE door to them with a smile. He took their coats and beckoned them through into the living room.

'I hope you were OK at the boathouse,' Ethan said pleasantly. Ella nodded, without looking him in the eye. 'Can I get you a drink?' he asked, heading towards the kitchen. 'Coffee or a coke or something?'

'Where's Charlie?' Alex asked.

'Sorry,' Ethan called from the other room, 'did you say you *would* like a drink?'

'I said, where's Charlie?' Alex said.

'He'll be down in a minute. He's just finishing his scales.' Ethan turned to Ella to explain. 'He's a very dedicated violinist. He's come on leaps and bounds in the past few months.'

Alex opened his mouth to say something but Ethan disappeared into the kitchen. Alex and Ella's eyes met. She could tell what he was thinking. And she agreed. This was pretty weird.

'Hello.' Sarah arrived in from the garden, holding a bunch of flowers in her hand. 'What a beautiful morning!' she said, kissing first Alex then Ella.

Again, Alex and Ella's eyes met. She knew that

his patience was running out. He strode out of the room and headed for the staircase. She decided to follow.

As they climbed the stairs, they heard the music. It was hard to believe it was a boy of nine playing it. The sound was very smooth and melodious but there was an extra quality – a depth of feeling.

Charlie was standing in the centre of the room, his back to the doorway. He carried on playing, apparently unaware of their presence. Ella watched the emotion flood into Alex's face.

The music ended. Charlie stood in position for a moment. It was as if the music had not quite left him. Alex and Ella waited. Finally, Charlie turned towards them.

'Alex. They said you were coming by.' Charlie's voice had almost no expression.

'Charlie . . .' Alex seemed struck dumb. As Charlie began packing away his things, Ella pushed Alex into the room. He walked up to Charlie and took his hands away from the violin case, catching them in his own and kneeling in front of him.

'I came back for you, Charlie,' Alex said, hugging his brother. 'I've missed you so much.'

Charlie looked up, over Alex's shoulder, at Ella. He seemed embarrassed. 'Did you like the music?' he asked.

'You're a very talented violinist,' Ella said.

'That's not what I asked,' he said. 'I asked about the music.'

She was taken aback. He had piercing eyes and did not speak like a nine-year-old.

'It was very haunting,' she said.

'Haunting.' He weighed the word. 'Yes, I like that. I made it up myself, you see. I'm Charlie, by the way,' he said, approaching her with his hand outstretched.

'Ella,' she said. 'I'm Alex's friend.'

'I like you,' he said, as if he had given the matter great thought. 'I like you heaps better than Carrie.'

He brushed past her and headed for the stairs. Ella watched Alex pull himself up and walk towards her. His face showed the confusion he was experiencing. What was happening?

They walked down the stairs to find Charlie had joined Ethan and Sarah in the living room. Charlie was sitting beside Ethan on the sofa and telling him about his new composition. 'I'm going to dedicate it to you,' he said decisively.

'Well now, since we're all together,' Ethan said, 'I think it's time we told Alex and Ella our news.'

'Yes!' Charlie grinned, wrapping his arm around Ethan's waist. Even Sarah seemed to be brimming with excitement.

Ella took Alex's hand. His eyes looked empty now.

'It's quite simple, really,' Ethan said. 'We're going to adopt Charlie.'

'We've already started the procedures,' Sarah added. 'Isn't it wonderful?'

Ella felt Alex's shock. She looked from Sarah to Charlie and then to Ethan. They looked like the perfect, all-American family. It was as if they had managed to erase the horrific events that had brought them together and created themselves anew.

Alex clenched her hand tightly and began pulling her towards the door. She was only too willing to follow.

'Alex! Ella! Wait. Don't go.' Sarah chased after them. 'What's wrong? Let's talk about this.'

Ella glanced back. Alex did not turn. He got into the car and started the engine.

'There's nothing for me here,' Alex said bitterly. 'We're leaving Oakport.'

She leaned over and kissed him sadly. He would never know it but he had saved her. Just in the nick of time.

CHAPTER VII

'I CAN'T BELIEVE what's happened to Charlie,' Alex said, as they packed up their things. 'We were so close.'

Ella caught his hands. 'You have to face it, Alex, he does seem to be happy with Sarah and Ethan.'

Alex shrugged. She could see tears welling in his eyes. 'I guess you're right.'

She clasped his hands tightly. 'Maybe it's time for us to get on with our own lives, Alex. We're just beginning.' She looked into his eyes. 'We're going to have such a wonderful time together.'

'Yes.' He smiled, but could not hold back the tears any longer. She pulled him close and let him cry into her shoulder.

It was hard for her to maintain the pretence of feeling calm when really she was terrified that he would change his mind about leaving Oakport. She knew now that she could not remain in the same town as Ethan Sawyer. As long as he was around, she would never be free to start over. Every time he looked at her, she became that frightened young girl again, alone in the snow. She had to move on – to break free of the memories, both good and bad, that flooded back every time she saw him or heard him speak.

'Hello! Anybody home?'

They both recoiled at Ethan's voice. In a moment, he was standing just behind Alex, smiling at Ella. 'I'm sorry to crash in like this, but I think we need to talk.'

There was no way Alex could hide from Ethan the fact that he had been crying. Ethan raised his hand to squeeze Alex's shoulder but, at the last moment, thought better of it.

'Sarah insisted I come,' Ethan said, sitting down on the sofa. 'She was upset that you stormed out of the house like that. We all were. I wanted to explain –'

'You may as well know, we're leaving town tonight,' Ella said.

Alex glanced at her in surprise, but Ethan seemed to take this news in his stride. 'I hope I can dissuade you from making that journey.'

He stood up and walked over to the bookshelf, picking up the photograph of him in the boat with Alex and Charlie.

'That was a great trip, remember, Alex?' he said, smiling. 'I guess they all were. Look, I know this adoption stuff has taken you by surprise. It is very sudden, after everything that's happened but Sarah and I feel it's really important to get things back on track.'

He held the photograph out to Alex. 'Look at him. He's smiling. And I want him to smile again.'

'Oh, he seems perfectly happy,' Alex said, bitterly.

'Alex, we're adopting Charlie because he needs people to take care of him ... You're seventeen – old enough to look after yourself. But not old enough to easily look after him.'

He sat down again, this time on the arm of the sofa Alex was sitting in. 'Stop by the house again tomorrow. Say around noon. Spend some quality time with Charlie ... just the two of you. We want you to stay a part of this family ... your family.'

Ella's heart and head were pounding. She had to put a stop to this. But how could she, without revealing to them both the depth of her feelings for Ethan?

Ethan put his arm around Alex's shoulder and hugged him. 'You coming back is a miracle, Alex. And miracles don't happen too often in Oakport. Don't throw this wonderful chance away. What do you say?'

Alex seemed incapable of arguing. His body seemed suddenly drained of all strength. As Ethan drew back his arm, Alex slumped against the corner of the sofa. His eyes were closed.

Ella looked at Ethan with alarm. 'What have you done?'

'Nothing,' Ethan said. 'He's very tired. It's been quite a day for him. For us all.'

He stood up again. This time, he moved differently – prowling around the room as if he owned the space.

'I think you should go,' Ella said, not quite as fiercely as she intended.

Ethan considered for a moment. 'I'm sure you wouldn't mind me staying for just one drink.'

Ella stood up. 'You shouldn't drink and drive. We don't want another tragedy, do we?'

They were standing face to face now. Ethan stared into her eyes. 'What could possibly happen to me?' he laughed. 'All right, I can see you're not in the mood for talk tonight. Well, I'll look forward to seeing you tomorrow. And while Charlie and Alex are getting reacquainted, maybe we should spend some time together alone.'

He turned and swaggered out of the boat-house. Ella looked at Alex, sprawled over the sofa. Her anger bubbled. She ran out after Ethan. He was about to climb into the car but stopped when he saw her.

'You can't keep doing this,' she cried. 'Every time I get myself back together you come after me and turn everything upside down again.'

He looked at her with amusement. 'That's hardly fair. This time you came to me. And you know, you're more beautiful than ever.' He traced the curve of her cheek with his finger.

She was still shaking long after he had reversed the car out on to the street and driven off into the night.

PRAGUE, 1782

A s she awaited an audience with her father – the emperor – Elisabeth's joy at returning to the palace was tinged with feelings of fear.

Her mother had prevented Elisabeth from seeing the emperor until she had cleaned herself up. In the meantime, she was conducting her own interrogation.

'It was Count de Savigny, yes? I saw you out on the castle wall.' There was a coldness to her mother's voice – a distance. Elisabeth knew what her mother must be thinking had happened. How her head would spin if she knew the truth.

A nervous, young maid hovered around them, smoothing the creases from a stunning sapphire-coloured dress. Elisabeth looked at herself in the mirror. She thought she looked older even though she had been absent only a matter of weeks. And yet there was a new flush to her. Although she had felt herself to be close to death, she looked more alive, more vibrant than she could remember.

'I'll wait for you in our chamber,' her mother said, slipping out of the room.

Elisabeth dipped her arms into the blue satin

dress the serving girl held over her and scooped up two necklaces from the jewellery box before her. One of the necklaces was gold, the other a string of sapphires. She was uncertain which to wear. The serving girl stepped back, waiting for the princess to decide.

Watching the way the gold necklace caught the light, Elisabeth thought of what story to tell the emperor. Should she let him believe, as her mother clearly did, that Eduard had simply deflowered her? What would life have in store for her then? The gossip would penetrate through the thick castle walls and bring shame upon the emperor and his family.

And yet . . . and yet. She held the string of sapphires close to her neck. Perhaps she could tell him the truth. Her father was a man of experience. He had travelled far and wide and was benefactor – and friend – to all manner of alchemists and adventurers. Perhaps he would know about such things as this. Perhaps he even knew of a cure.

'I'll wear the sapphires,' she decided. The serving girl stepped forward to help her fasten the chain. Elisabeth couldn't help but notice the swan's arch of the girl's neck. She followed the arch down to where it met her narrow shoulders. The now familiar hunger surged inside her . . .

No! Not here! Not now. She tried to still the hunger but it was too powerful. Before she knew it, she had the girl's throat in her grip and was biting down into her neck . . .

Breathless, she let the girl's body fall to the carpet. Now what? She looked in the mirror once again and lifted a lace handkerchief to wipe away the blood around her lips. She caught herself in the process. There was no turning back. She realized then that she must leave the castle for ever.

She flung open the door of the chamber and ran out into the corridor. She heard her parents' voices but hurried past their room, hurtling down the great staircase and across the hall. The solid wood doors were impossibly heavy but her strength was gaining all the time. She tugged them open and charged out into the cool night.

As she neared the gates, she heard a familiar voice. 'It's all right. I have made plans.'

She looked up and saw a carriage and horses, waiting just beyond the gate. The guard looked sadly at her but opened the gate all the same. She clasped his hands for an instant but there was no more time to lose. The carriage door opened and another hand reached out to help her inside. As the door closed behind her, the horses tore off into the night.

She turned towards Eduard. He was clean and dressed in new clothes, looking more elegant and handsome than ever before. She scanned his face for signs of anger but found none.

*

She awoke from a deep sleep to find herself in his arms. The carriage had come to a halt and she looked out through the window to see a magnificent castle bathed in the soft moonlight.

'This will be your new home,' Eduard said, lifting her down from the carriage. 'Come inside.'

He took her hand and led her into the hallway. A few servants paused from their duties to smile and call out in welcome. They seemed pleased that their master had returned. There was an air of warmth and informality about the place.

'Come,' he said, leading her up the stairs and along a corridor. They came to a door, just slightly ajar. He urged her to push it fully open. She did so and found herself inside a ballroom. Around the edges of the dance floor were candles flickering atop all manner of candelabra.

'Now, dance with me,' he said.

'There's no music.'

But suddenly, she heard the first stirrings of her favourite waltz. She glanced around the room, seeking out the source of the music. She could see no one playing. Her eyes returned to Eduard and she thought she understood.

Gratefully, she fell into his arms and let him lead her to the centre of the floor. She lost herself in the music and the thrill of his touch, feeling her heart flood with joy. The light of the candles seemed to dance around her. She smiled.

'I love you.' Shocked, she looked back into his

deep, green eyes. This time, she really wasn't sure if he had spoken the words or if her mind was simply playing tricks upon her.

CHAPTER VIII

'I HOPE I got your size right,' Ethan said, smiling. 'Go on, Alex. Aren't you going to try yours on?'

Alex looked at Ethan as if he had asked him to walk on fire. He glared at the Rollerblades, sitting inside their box. But Charlie had already buckled his up and Ethan was helping him on with his pads.

'Now, Charlie,' he said, 'the guy at the store told me you have to promise not to do this without wearing pads, you understand?' Charlie nodded and raced off down the road.

Ethan watched him go. 'You'd better get a move on, Alex, or Charlie will be out of sight!' Ethan turned to Ella. 'I'll just grab my car keys and we can get going too.'

'Where are you going with him?' Alex asked, buckling his blades.

'To the gallery,' Ella said.

'The gallery? You're not seriously interested in his photographs, are you?'

'Don't worry about me, Alex. Just give it your best shot with Charlie, OK?'

He nodded and leaned forward to kiss her. As he did so, he lost his balance. They both laughed.

'I guess these blades are going to take some getting used to,' Alex said and skated off after Charlie.

Ethan reappeared with the keys. 'All set?' he asked Ella.

She nodded and walked over to Ethan's car.

As they drove away, Ethan slipped a CD into the car stereo. 'How long's it been?' he said. 'Thirty years? Forty?'

She shrugged.

He shot her a smile. 'Don't say you're not pleased to see me?'

She shrugged.

'You're looking very well,' he continued. 'This Ella suits you.'

He looked almost the same as he had the first time she had met him – a little older, rather more American than European. Blue eyes instead of green but equally intense. His hair was the same colour and was a similar length, falling down to the base of his neck.

He smiled at her. 'We've got a lot of catching up to do.'

She wanted to hate him – out of loyalty to Alex, and to make him pay for the past. It was easier said than done. There were good memories as well as bad. She felt her pulse quicken and her fear give way to a sense of anticipation.

Ethan turned off the road into a small parking

lot, beside the lake. He brought the car to a standstill.

'How far are we from the boathouse?' Ella asked.

'It's on the other side of the lake,' he said. 'This place was a boathouse too. But we've made some changes inside . . .'

'I thought you were just exhibiting here.'

'Sarah and I own it,' Ethan explained. 'Come on inside!' He opened the door for her.

Ella walked into the exhibition room. It was large, empty of furniture, and wood from floor to ceiling. It was as stark as it could be, perfectly setting off the photographs that hung on its walls. Like the boathouse, the building opened straight out on to the lake.

Ethan led her from one picture to the next, telling her about the locations and the way he'd achieved particular effects – the story behind the pictures.

'You've come a long way,' she said, adding with a smile, 'since Paris!'

He caught the joke and laughed with her. 'I think I was a little avant-garde even for the French.'

A few more people strolled into the gallery. When they realized Ethan was the photographer, they'd start up a conversation. But Ella could see that Ethan was not in the mood for this. It did not surprise her when he took her arm and led her to the door.

'Let's go and get some lunch,' he said. 'I want some time alone with you.'

'Something's bothering you,' Ethan said over lunch, 'tell me about it.'

'I want you to make peace with Alex,' she said.

'Talk to *him*,' Ethan said, reaching for the lobster tail. 'He's the one who insists on making me the enemy.'

'Does he have any reason to do that?' she asked. Their eyes met.

'What are you accusing me of?' Ethan asked.

'Alex says that you murdered his parents.'

Ethan closed his hand over Ella's. 'It was an accident,' he said. 'Oh, I was stupid, pig-headed – well, you know what I'm like! I should have paid more attention to the storm reports.'

Ella looked deep into his eyes, trying to decide if this was the truth. He returned her stare.

'Look, I saved Charlie, didn't I?' he said. 'And I looked for Alex for hours. I didn't know he'd swum to safety.'

She wanted to believe him so very much.

'Why would I jeopardize everything I have with Sarah by killing her brother and his wife? What could I possibly have to gain?'

'You really love her then?' Ella had forgotten all about Sarah. She felt a flash of guilt at hearing her name.

When she glanced up at him, he was smiling at

her. It was not the smile he had offered to the people at the gallery. It was a genuine smile, full of warmth, full of love.

'I've missed you,' he said.

She turned and looked at him, filled with fear and sorrow and longing. And then his lips met hers and she forgot everything but the longing.

CHAPTER IX

SARAH WAS STANDING in the doorway as Ethan's car pulled up at Shadow Street. 'You were gone such a long time,' she said as he kissed her hello.

'I took Ella to the gallery and then we got some lunch. We started talking and, well ... I guess we have a lot in common.'

Sarah smiled weakly at Ella. Ella felt uncomfortable. She was about to ask if Charlie and Alex were still out blading, when she heard a trail of violin notes from upstairs.

'Is Alex up with Charlie?' she asked.

'Oh no.' Sarah shook her head. 'They got back ages ago. Charlie went up to his room and Alex drove back out to the boathouse.'

Alex opened the door to her but said nothing.

'I'm sorry I'm so late,' she said.

'Gee, that's all right,' he came right back at her. 'I can quite understand why you'd want to spend the afternoon with my psychotic uncle.'

She hadn't expected him to be this angry. 'How was your day?'

'Great, thanks,' he said sarcastically. 'My little brother was on excellent form – just a joy to be with. He's so happy with his new life with Ethan and Sarah. What does it matter to him that his parents are six feet under or whether I'm alive or dead?'

Ella sat down at the other end of the sofa. He had every right to be upset.

'Nice Rollerblades, huh?' Alex lifted the blades and spun the wheels. 'Uncle Ethan's spoiling us, don't you think?'

Something snapped inside Ella. She felt guilty, angry and confused. 'Give him a break. You can't blame Ethan for everything that's happened. You have to face the fact that Charlie *is* happy with them. Maybe he should stay here while we get on with our own lives . . .'

'Only it isn't exactly a life, is it?' Alex said. 'Let's not forget that my name's on a gravestone out there in the churchyard. Oh and by now, I've probably been given another funeral in England. So when you come to think of it, I don't have too much of a life to be getting on with.'

He stormed out on to the deck. Ella followed. She tried to push down her anger. She had to keep calm.

'He told me about the accident, Alex,' she said, reaching for his shoulder. 'He admits he should have brought the boat back earlier. He feels really guilty. He did come back to save you but he couldn't find you. It was misty.'

Alex shook his head. He would not accept this

version of events. She looked into his eyes, hoping in vain.

'Have you finished?' he asked, coldly. 'Does the defence for Ethan Sawyer rest its case?'

She was incensed. 'I'm not defending him! I'm just . . .'

'You seem quite convinced by his side of the story,' he snapped, shrugging her hands from his shoulders.

It was growing dark, the lack of daylight intensified by gathering storm clouds. Ella glanced down into the dark waters of the lake.

She tried once more to change his mind. 'But when you think about it, Alex, what *he* is saying fits with your version of events. It isn't a question of sides . . .'

Alex would not give in. 'He identified my body for the police, remember? He told them that yes, it was me lying on that slab . . . when I was upstate, in a hospital bed being fed soup. He organized my funeral while I was buying a plane ticket to England. How does he explain that?'

She had no answer for him. She felt a chill come over her. It wasn't just the first icy droplets of rain. Ethan hadn't told her the truth . . . at least, not the whole truth. There was still more she needed to know.

'I . . . have . . . to go.' She darted inside. The keys to the Thunderbird were on the table. She scooped them up and raced out of the door, leaving her coat and bag on the sofa. Alex ran after her. It had started to rain.

'NO!' he called, racing to the car. But she was too quick for him. Before he reached her, she stamped down hard on the throttle and sped away along the road.

Sarah answered the door. She was clearly surprised to see Ella again. 'What do you want?'

'I have to see Ethan,' Ella said.

'He's rather busy just now,' Sarah began but in a moment Ethan himself came to the door.

'You look awful,' he said. 'Come in and get dry.'

She shook her head. 'No. You come with me.'

'Ethan,' she heard Sarah say, 'what exactly's going on?'

Ella turned and walked back towards the car. Ethan chased after her. He had scarcely fastened his safety belt as she drove away at high speed.

'Where are we going?' he asked.

'You're not the only one who can spring a surprise,' she said, enjoying the feeling of power.

He leaned back against the seat and looked out of the window. Ella grew tired of the game. She needed answers.

'Why did you say the body they found was Alex's?' she asked.

He took a moment. She turned, expecting him to be smiling, smugly. She was shocked to see the way he looked – scared and doubtful, vulnerable even. She was not accustomed to seeing him like this.

'I really thought it was Alex,' he said. 'The face . . . the face was too badly . . . damaged. You couldn't tell. But he was Alex's height and build. He had long, dark hair. Most of his clothes were torn up . . . except the scraps of his shirt. I thought I recognized the shirt . . .'

As he broke off, Ella stole another glance at him. Tears were streaming down his face.

'Ella, watch the road!' he cried.

As she turned, she saw that the car was veering perilously close to the cliff edge. She tried to bring it under control but they were travelling much too fast and the road was narrow and winding. They were heading towards a deep precipice.

Alarmed, she wrestled with the wheel, managing to pull the car away from the edge just in the nick of time. She slowed the Thunderbird and, as the road widened, brought the car to a standstill.

'Now what?' he asked.

'I want you to come back to the boathouse,' she told him. 'I want you to tell Alex what you've told me. I want an end to this feud tonight.'

The boathouse door was ajar and the floorboards nearby were wet with rain. The hurricane lamp was unlit and the clouds blocked out all light from the moon. As her eyes adjusted, Ella could see that the living room was empty.

She was about to call out to Alex when she noticed that the doors to the deck were open. The flimsy curtains flapped like streamers in the wind, spraying the room with droplets of rain.

She stepped out on to the deck. Her foot came up against something soft but firm. She glanced down and realized that there was a human body stretched out at her feet.

Just then, the moon broke free of the storm clouds and the boathouse was bathed in light. Ella recognized the body below her. It was the girl who had recognized Alex outside the party. She looked up, helplessly, at Ella. At the very least she was unconscious. Instinctively, Ella lifted the damp strands of hair and saw the puncture marks on the girl's neck.

There was a crash in the living room. Ella turned. The hurricane lamp had fallen to the floor. Alex stood above the mess of broken glass. He moved towards her, as if sleepwalking. His shirt was torn and spattered with blood.

'Why here?' Ella asked, numbly. 'Why did you bring her here?'

'I couldn't help it. She saw us out blading. She must have followed me.'

'You've taken too much blood, Alex. I warned you . . .'

'I was angry,' he said. He was shaking.

'I think you've killed her.' Ella stepped inside

out of the rain. As she did so, Ethan, who had been standing beside her on the deck, crouched down to inspect the body.

'What's he doing here?'

'It's OK,' Ella told Alex. 'He understands.'

She saw Alex make the connection. The pieces to the jigsaw came together in his head.

'She's going to be all right,' Ethan said. 'We just need to get her out of here.'

But Alex just stood there, staring at Ethan. 'You're one of us,' he said. 'You're a vampire.'

CHAPTER X

THEY LEFT THE still unconscious girl at the side of a road, leading out of the woods. In the morning, someone was sure to find her. There would be no way of tracing what had happened back to the boathouse.

'But what happens when she remembers that she followed me here?' Alex asked.

'She won't remember anything for a few days,' Ethan said. 'And when she does, it will all be confused. Besides, who would believe her? Everyone around here thinks you're dead.'

Listening to them, Ella felt a sudden sense of relief that the truth was out in the open. She wondered which of them was the more surprised – Alex at discovering that Ethan was a vampire, or Ethan at discovering that Alex was.

Back at the boathouse, Alex went to clean himself up, leaving Ella and Ethan alone in the living room. Alex was wide awake now and seemed ashamed of what he had done.

Ethan smiled. 'So, you have an apprentice of your own.'

'You should go,' Ella said, abruptly. She didn't want to talk to Ethan about Alex.

Ethan did not move.

'Sarah will be worried,' Ella said.

Ethan glanced at the clock. 'I suppose you're right.' He held out his hand. 'Walk with me to the car.'

She followed, anxious to see him go. But as soon as they were outside, he grabbed her by the shoulders, bringing her face to face with him.

'What are you doing with Alex?' he said harshly.

'I love him,' she cried, trying to wriggle out of his grip. She couldn't.

'No.' Ethan shook his head. 'It isn't love.'

Ella looked angrily into Ethan's eyes. How did he know how she felt about Alex? What right did he have to storm back into her life and tell her whom she loved and whom she did not love.

'Don't you see?' he continued. 'It isn't over between us.'

'It has to be. I'm with Alex now. And you're with Sarah.'

'I don't love *her*. How could I feel about her the way I do about you? Sarah and Alex are like children. You and I . . . we're different. We've seen so much, been through so much *together*.'

That was true. They had shared a lot of history. *You can never escape from me. You can never run away from what you've become.* He had spoken those words 200 years ago. Then, they had seemed only a threat. But now, she knew it was true.

She had spent two hundred years running from him and from the way he lived – taking whatever, whoever he wanted and never mind the cost. Leaving a trail of death and destruction behind him. She had been sure that there was another way, had taught herself moderation. But now everything was uncertain again.

She thought she had found a new beginning in Alex. So much so, that she had brought him back from the realms of the dead. But even by bringing him back – making him a vampire – she had only succeeded in creating another monster. She had tried to teach him to control his hunger, just as she had taught herself. But it was no good. Alex's bloodlust showed every sign of being as insatiable as Eduard's. Maybe that was just the way it had to be. Maybe it was time for her to accept that there was no escape from blood. Death and destruction were just a part of the deal.

She looked up into Ethan's eyes. As she did so, their blueness seemed to fade, replaced by the emerald-green of Eduard de Savigny.

'We'll talk again soon,' he said. 'You'll see I'm right.' He started up the car and disappeared into the night.

Ella found Alex out on the deck, sitting as still as a statue. The rain had died away to no more than a drizzle but there was still a cold wind. He did not seem to feel it, even though his shirt was unbuttoned and flapped in the breeze. She was reminded of the first time she had seen him, watching the tide coming in on a beach thousands of miles away.

'So, he's the one. The Count you were telling me about.' There was no mistaking the bitterness in Alex's expression.

She nodded, biting her lip.

'He made you a vampire two hundred years ago and now he's here. Did you know he would be?'

'When we arrived, I . . . I sensed he might.'

Alex nodded. 'That's why you were so edgy about coming to Oakport.' She was shocked that he had noticed.

'I was scared about what would happen,' Ella said. She realized that she was scared now. Alex was slipping away from her and she was powerless to prevent it. She would only bring him pain. Maybe, if she left with Ethan, that would finally bring the Culler family a sense of peace.

'I'm leaving Oakport.'

Ella was stunned. She had been about to say the very same words.

'There's nothing for me here,' Alex continued. 'I'll leave in the morning. You can keep the car.'

For a second she considered suggesting that they left town immediately, together. But why was she kidding herself? It was over.

'I love you, Alex.'

He turned to look at her sadly and shrugged.

She could not blame him if he did not believe her. She could feel the tears pricking her eyes. Suddenly she couldn't bear to cry in front of him. She ran inside, into the bedroom and threw herself down on the bed. Why had she allowed this to happen? Why hadn't she just told Alex about Ethan as soon as she'd realized? In trying to protect him, she had only hurt him more.

She lay there in the darkness, wondering if Alex would come inside. If only he would give her a chance to explain. But what more could she say? Filled with despair, she submitted to sleep.

In the first moment of waking she felt refreshed and relaxed. She could feel the warmth of sunlight through the curtains. Opening her eyes, she turned to her side, just hoping. But Alex wasn't there.

An echo of the sadness she had felt the previous evening came to her. But it was displaced by another emotion. Sleep had brought her to a new decision. There was no more time to waste. She leaped out of bed.

The living room was empty. Maybe Alex had spent the whole night out on the deck. Ella approached the doors that led out to the lake. They were fastened. The deck was empty.

She looked into the bathroom. Empty. The kitchen. Nothing. Filled with panic, she pulled open the front door. The car was still there. Then she remembered him telling her that he'd leave her the car. Her heart was pounding as she shut the door again. It was then that she noticed the postcard on the table, weighted down by a ring of keys.

The card was picture side up. She picked it up. The picture of the small fishing port brought back a rush of memories of their travels. They'd eaten clam chowder that night, in an inn on the ocean-front. The memories flooded back. When she finally summoned the courage to turn over the card and read it, the sight of his spiky writing was too much to bear.

Be happy, love, Alex.

Her tears spilled down on to the card, splattering the ink until the letters sprawled and twisted and were quite unreadable. Where had he gone? She had to find him. She had to tell him that it was him she loved, not Ethan. Even if he wouldn't take her back, she had to let him know.

She hammered on the door at Shadow Street for ages before anyone answered.

'I'm sorry, I was practising,' Charlie said. He was still holding his violin and bow.

'Is Alex here?'

Charlie shook his head.

'Was he here before?'

'Not this morning. Would you like to come inside? You look kind of upset.'

'Is Ethan here? Or Sarah?'

'Ethan's at his gallery and Sarah's gone into town.'

'I . . . have to find Alex . . .' Ella stammered.

'Sorry,' Charlie shrugged, 'I can't help you. Are you sure you don't want to come in?'

Standing there, wondering where to go next, Ella's eyes flashed over the photographs in the living room. There was one she hadn't noticed before. She darted inside. The scene the picture portrayed was familiar to her. It was the view from the living room of the boathouse. There was the deck, and beyond it the lake. There was the boat . . . the boat! It hadn't been there this morning. Alex must have taken it. Exhilarated by her discovery, she darted out of the house without offering Charlie any explanation. She had to get back to the boathouse. Nothing else mattered now.

When she arrived back at the boathouse, her exhilaration soon turned to frustration. The boat *had* gone but where had Alex taken it? She set off to search, on foot this time.

As she ran along the lakeside, her mind flooded with memories of Alex. The first time she had seen him, watching the waves. The first time they had kissed, alone on the beach. The terrible moment when his motorbike had veered off the cliff road and down . . . And then his smile as she had woken him from the sleep of death. She *had* to find him.

*

It was late afternoon when she finally returned to the boathouse after a long and futile search. She had not glimpsed the boat or Alex once. She felt bitterly disappointed.

There was so much she wanted to tell him. How it was always the same with Eduard. They'd come together for a while – he was exciting, there was no denying that. But to him, being a vampire was an excuse to take whatever he wanted – whoever he wanted – whatever the damage he wrought. And how he took life – or whatever this was – on the run.

Ella was tired of running. Eduard had told her that it was the only way. But she knew differently now. Since meeting Alex, a thousand new possibilities seemed to have opened up for her. With him, all the cynicism that had built up over two hundred years had disappeared. She saw things freshly through his eyes. He might be a child compared to her and Ethan, but he had plenty to teach her just the same. She loved him – more than she would ever have thought possible. And now she missed him more than ever.

As she came to the door, she noticed a box propped to one side of the doorway. It hadn't been there that morning. She opened the door and carried it inside. Although large, it was quite light.

She carried it to the sofa and lifted the lid. There was a thick package wrapped in tissue paper. It rustled as she lifted it out from the box.

As the tissue fell away, she gasped. It was a green, silk dress – just like the one she had worn to that ball all those years before.

There was another package in the box. As if in a trance, she laid the dress carefully on the sofa and reached down into the box. A pair of emerald satin shoes tumbled out of their tissue wrapping. Spellbound, she dipped her feet into the slippers. They fitted perfectly.

At the very bottom of the box she found an envelope. As she lifted it closer, she saw that it was marked only 'E'. She took out the card inside and read the familiar writing: *What do you think? Not a bad likeness, is it? Wear it tonight and come to the gallery at eight.*

She set the card down and picked up the dress. Her thoughts were confused. She had to find Alex – had to focus on him not this dress, these slippers . . .

But suddenly, she found herself fastening the dress. She approached the mirror nervously, her eyes half-closed. The spell was complete.

She began pushing her hair into a different style. Now, when she examined the reflection, she no longer saw Ella Ryder. Princess Elisabeth had returned. All her thoughts turned to the ball that awaited her. She was impatient for the dance to begin. Impatient and nervous and excited.

CHAPTER XI

THE DOOR TO the gallery was open. She heard faint notes of music. As she stepped inside the music gained momentum.

She walked on through the hallway. Ahead of her, candles flickered. The light drew her on, until she was standing in the centre of the gallery. There were candlesticks and candelabra all around the edges of the room creating a moat of light.

The pictures she had viewed before had been removed from the walls. In their place were mirrors, of all shapes and sizes, reflecting the candles. As she struggled to distinguish the real candles from their reflections, she caught sight of him. He was dressed in a dark suit with tails. His face was covered by a mask.

'May I have this dance?' He held out his hand to her, but as she moved forward to take it, he appeared from another direction entirely. She realized that she had been watching him in the mirror. Now she trembled as he circled his arms around her.

She had not danced this way for a long time but her feet seemed to remember the steps. It was as if he had managed to turn time right back to the beginning.

As the music slowed she felt a sudden sense of sadness. He pulled her towards him and threw off the mask. His blond hair tumbled down around his neck.

She looked nervously into his eyes. He hesitated for a moment – his eyes taking in the way she looked in the dress, before returning to her face. His face came towards her then and she did not resist. His lips were upon hers and she reached out her hands to the back of his head and pulled him closer still.

They were still kissing as the waltz ended. As he drew away, he planted tiny kisses on her cheek and neck. She shivered, remembering what his kisses had brought her to before. But what more could he do to her now? Now they were equal. She smiled up at him as they began to dance again.

'What would you have done if I hadn't come?' she asked.

'I knew you would. You want this as much as I do.'

He was right. Everything else was only a distraction, an avoidance of the truth. The truth was simple. They should be together. Nothing else mattered.

She rested her head on his shoulder as they waltzed slowly around the room. But then, suddenly, she saw Charlie. At first she thought it was her imagination as he walked hesitantly towards her through the pool of light.

Ethan smiled. 'Charlie. We've been waiting for you.'

Ella was puzzled. What did he mean? Why had they been waiting for Charlie?

'Charlie's coming with us,' Ethan said, as if reading her mind.

'What? Why?' She was filled with confusion.

Ethan slipped his arm from her and moved towards Charlie. He stood behind him, resting his hands on the boy's shoulders.

'We're going to be a family.' He began stroking Charlie's hair. 'I have such plans for him.'

Ella suddenly felt cold. The spell was broken. She noticed with horror that Charlie's eyes were empty as glass.

'He'll make a better vampire than you or I,' Ethan said. 'He'll be a legend.'

Ella felt sick. This wasn't about love. It was about power. Nothing had changed. How could she have deceived herself? How could she have let him trick her once again?

'Ethan, I don't want Charlie to come with us. Let's just go together.'

He shook his head. 'Do you know how long I've been preparing this? I almost lost ... everything.'

'What do you mean?'

'When the boat went down,' he said, 'the water was pouring towards me. I only just made it to the dinghy in time. And then I had to rescue Charlie. I couldn't lose him then, after all those months of preparation.'

She held herself together, determined not to show her feelings. It was far from easy.

'You said it was an accident . . .'

'It *was* an accident,' Ethan said. 'But, of course, I saw the advantages. With no parents, no other family, there were no further obstacles. The plan could be accomplished.'

Ella glanced at Charlie. During all this, he remained quite impassive. Ethan had worked some kind of spell over him – just the way he had sent Alex to sleep that night at the boathouse. Just the way he had brought her here.

'So you left his parents to drown?' she said. 'And Alex.' She found it harder still to keep the emotion out of her voice.

He looked deep in thought, as if he had returned to that moment and was going through it all again.

'I thought about saving him. But it would only have complicated things. He would have stood in my way.'

'So you just left him there?'

'None of this matters now,' he said, pulling her towards him. 'I've made plans. We leave tonight . . .'

She drew back, slipping out of his arms. 'No,' she said, terrified but determined. 'I'm not coming.'

'Don't be foolish,' he said. 'You have no choice.'

She tensed her body, ready to run.

'Don't even think of it. This time, you won't get away from me.'

Perhaps he was right. Perhaps she should go with him, if only to protect Charlie. No. She would do everything in her power to stop him taking Charlie. She owed it to Alex. If only Alex were there now.

'Alex!' Charlie's voice called out.

Ella stared at Charlie, wondering how he had tuned into her thoughts. His eyes were fixed on the doors behind Ethan, the doors that gave out on to the dark waters of the lake.

She followed Charlie's gaze and saw Alex standing outside the window. Ethan saw him too. Suddenly Alex was in the room, standing before Ethan.

'Well, isn't this nice?' Ethan sneered. 'All vampires together!'

'All?' Alex faltered, staring at Charlie. 'What have you done?'

'We have to save Charlie!' Ella cried.

'You won't stop me! No one will stop me.' Ethan grabbed Charlie and held him in a vicelike grip.

Instinctively, Alex threw himself towards them. As he did so, he knocked one of the tall candlesticks. As it fell forward, the candles tumbled out and rolled across the floor towards the edges of the room. Ella watched them scatter in different directions. She ought to extinguish the flames but how could she reach them all in time?

Charlie was still caught in Ethan's grip. Alex struggled to free him but Ethan's hold only grew tighter. Ella saw the light glint on Ethan's teeth as his mouth lowered towards Charlie's neck.

'No!' she cried.

But her cries were drowned out by an explosion of noise and light. As the bright flash of the first fire gave way to thick black smoke, Ella could smell the stench of chemicals. The candles must have ignited some of Ethan's processing materials. She was submerged in a dark fog, broken only by flying glass as around her the mirrors caught fire and cracked.

She collapsed helplessly into a heap as the boathouse began to shake. She heard a terrible crash beside her. Looking up, she saw that the roof was starting to cave in. She had to get out to the lake. They all had to . . .

Her heart began to pound. She called out for Alex but had to close her mouth to stop the smoke from coming in. Petrified, she crawled across the floor, praying that she was moving in the right direction and not back into the heart of the fire.

As her hands reached the water, she felt a sudden rush of joy, but it soon died away, replaced by more practical concerns. She *had* to get inside the boat. She rolled inside, just as a new breath of fire lashed out at her. Quickly, she untied the boat from its mooring and took the oars in her hands. Her grip was poor but the current itself seemed to be carrying her away from the boathouse.

She looked up at the charred remains, searching frantically for the others. 'Alex!' she cried. The smoke had penetrated deep down into her throat and the cry sent a searing pain right through her. It didn't matter. The only thing that mattered was whether they were safe.

At last, two figures emerged from the smoke. She saw Charlie first. And behind him came Alex. Ella's heart lifted. It was a miracle. She steered the boat back towards the deck. Alex and Charlie staggered to the edge of the deck and jumped down beside her.

The building was utterly consumed by fire. Where was Ethan? Ella's blood ran cold. After everything he had done to her – to them all – she still felt a wrench of pain as she saw the billowing smoke.

Suddenly, he appeared. He looked weak and fearful. She had never seen him this way.

'Come on!' she cried instinctively. 'Get into the boat!'

He looked at her strangely. It was as if he did not know her. He seemed unable to move, rooted to the spot. Ella had to turn her eyes as the last remains of the ceiling caved in and he was crushed under a blanket of fire.

She screamed. Alex grabbed the oars and began rowing them away from shore. Once they had gone a safe distance, he let the oars drop and took Ella in his arms. Tears were streaming down her face and she was shaking.

'It's OK,' Alex whispered. 'Everything's going to be OK.'

Ella pulled Alex's face towards her and kissed him. It had taken this to bring them back together. Now, she never wanted them to be apart again. She tried to tell him but he hushed her. Well, there would be time enough to tell him how she felt.

They moored the boat further up the lake. She could hear the sirens as fire engines made their way through the night. It was too late, she thought ruefully. Too late for Ethan Sawyer.

Even as she saw the flames take their final hold on the deck, Ella found it hard to believe that he was gone. And that he was never coming back. She felt a surge of regret. She had loved him. She could no longer deny it.

And yet, he had been a savage man. Evil. His final actions on earth had shown that. She turned to Charlie. His neck was still red where Ethan had held him in his deathly grip. Charlie smiled up at her. He looked different somehow, as if the shock and terror had broken Ethan's spell.

'Thank you,' he said. 'You saved us.'

Ella felt Alex's arms circling her waist. Felt his

lips brush against her neck. She leaned back against him, her eyes lifting towards the dark sky. Though she was still shaking and full of fear, she knew that there was one thing she could be sure of – Alex loved her. And she loved him. And, whatever other dragons lay in wait for them, they would face them and fight them. Together.

Touched by the Vampire

For Kim

CHAPTER I

OAKPORT, MAINE

A WIDE SHOT OF the churchyard filled the TV screen. The reporter – a thin man in a suit – negotiated a path through the graves. As he crouched down among the grave stones, the camera narrowed in on him until his face filled the whole screen. He then began to speak:

'Tragedy first struck the Culler family just over a year ago when local physician, Dr Adam Culler, and his wife, Charlotte, were drowned at sea during a freak storm. They were out sailing with their sons Alex, seventeen, and Charlie, eleven. Also on the boat was Adam Culler's brother-in-law, Ethan Sawyer.'

The camera panned slowly across the inscriptions on the gravestones:

Adam Culler, 1952–1995. Beloved husband of Charlotte and father of Alexander and Charles . . .

Charlotte Baines Culler, 1954–1995 . . .

Alexander Culler, 1978–1995. Son of Adam and Charlotte. 'In their death they were not divided' . . .

Ethan Sawyer, 1962–1996. Mourned by his wife Sarah. 'Brief is life, but love is long' . . .

The reporter continued: 'Sawyer survived the storm and rescued his nephew Charlie. Alex Culler was thought to have perished alongside his parents. Indeed, a body discovered days after the incident was identified by Ethan Sawyer as that of his oldest nephew.

'After the funeral for Alex Culler and his parents, Charlie Culler went to live with Ethan and Sarah Sawyer, his aunt and uncle. Sources within the community recall that the three responded to the tragedy by becoming a tight-knit family unit. It seems that Ethan Sawyer, an acclaimed photographer with a lakeside gallery, soon became a second father to young Charlie.

'A year after the accident, the family received the joyous news that Alex Culler was alive. Traumatized by the loss of his parents, he had spent time recuperating in England. In fact it was only six weeks ago that Alex returned to Oakport to be reunited with his brother, uncle and aunt. With him, Alex brought his glamorous new girlfriend – Ella Ryder.

'But fate had not yet finished with the Culler

and Sawyer families. Just as their story appeared to have reached a happy conclusion, tragedy struck once again.

'One month ago, Ethan Sawyer was killed in a fire at his lakeside gallery. It is thought that Sawyer died in the act of rescuing his nephew Charlie. Alex and Charlie Culler and Alex's girlfriend, Ella, all survived the accident, although we can only imagine the psychological wounds they bear. Alex and Ella are currently living in the family's old boathouse on the lake, while Charlie remains in the care of his aunt, Sarah Sawyer.

'As a community, we must allow them all time to grieve. And yet, one question remains. Now that we know Alex Culler is alive and that Ethan Sawyer incorrectly identified the body of his nephew, who is the body in Alex's grave?

'By the end of today, we'll be one step closer to solving that mystery, because the grave is being exhumed and a battery of tests will be carried out on the mystery corpse.'

Click. The picture contracted to a tiny square and was gone. Ella set down the remote control on top of the TV.

'What were you watching?' Alex asked as he entered the room. He had been showering and was wrapped in a towel.

'Nothing,' Ella said. She felt guilty lying to him, but it would be worse telling him the truth.

'I'll just get dressed and then I guess we'd

better get over to Shadow Street. This won't be an easy day for Sarah or Charlie.'

As he padded out of the room again, she instinctively reached for the remote control. She weighed it in her palm, but couldn't bring herself to switch the TV back on. She was torn between immersing herself in the news coverage and trying to ignore it. It was strange hearing these strangers talk about her life and the people closest to her . . .

Alex's glamorous new girlfriend . . . It was like being two people at once. One was in the middle of it all while the other watched with cool interest from the sidelines.

Ella wondered how Alex felt. He seemed to be coping well, being strong for his family. She admired the way he had rallied around Sarah and Charlie, after all the pain he had been through himself. There had been no love lost between Alex and his uncle Ethan, at the end. And yet, Alex knew that both Sarah and Charlie had loved the man and that now they mourned him.

The only thing . . . Ella tried to stop the thought from surfacing again, but she couldn't . . . The only thing that Alex hadn't allowed for was that she was also in mourning. After all, she had known the man who had called himself Ethan for far longer than the others. Perhaps he was a bad man. Certainly he could be cruel. Sometimes she had thought him evil. But that hadn't stopped her from loving him.

Alex could not accept that. He hadn't said as much but she knew that whilst it was all right for Charlie and Sarah to have loved Ethan in life and mourn him in death, Alex would see her own grief as betrayal. So she put on a brave face and tried to submerge the tidal wave of emotion that arose whenever her thoughts strayed to the other man. But the more she tried to deny her feelings, the deeper they took root inside her head. It was driving a wedge between her and Alex and she could see no way to prevent it.

'All set?'

She turned to see his smiling face. He looked shiny and new with wax in his hair and a fresh set of clothes. For once, she really felt two hundred years older than him. Blind to her feelings, he took her hand and led her out of the boathouse and towards the waiting car.

CHAPTER II

THEY HAD ALMOST driven past the churchyard when Alex caught sight of a figure in the rear-view mirror.

'Isn't that Sarah? What's she doing here?'

He slowed the car and then shifted it into reverse. Ella looked over at the woman approaching the church gates. Surely she was too old and frail to be Sarah. But grief had taken its toll on Alex's aunt and, on second glance, Ella was certain that it was her.

'We'd better follow her,' Alex said.

'What about the TV crews?'

'We can handle them. I'm not sure that she can.'

They parked the car and followed Sarah. As they made their way around the side of the church, they caught sight of the reporters swarming around the graves.

Sarah's steps were slow and uneven. Ella and Alex were soon close to catching up with her.

'Sarah,' Alex called softly.

She turned. In her hands she clutched a bunch of red roses, tied with ribbon. She smiled at Alex and Ella. It was a strange smile – as if it had been ages since she had seen them, rather than hours.

Although soft, Alex's call had alerted one of the cameramen. He turned his lens in their direction and began shooting. The reporter he was working with caught on to what was happening and began striding towards them. The agility with which he moved was impressive, like a jungle beast closing in on its kill.

Even as he moved, he turned to face the camera and began speaking.

'As the exhumation continues, we've been joined in the churchyard by Sarah Sawyer, grieving widow of Ethan Sawyer, along with Alex Culler and his girlfriend, Ella Ryder. Folks, can I get a few words with you?'

They were trapped. Alex placed a protective arm around Sarah's shoulders. Ella grasped the woman's trembling hand.

'I just . . . wanted to bring him some . . . flowers,' Sarah stammered.

'This must be a very difficult time for you.' The reporter assumed a tone of exquisite sympathy. 'So, any thoughts on whose body is in that grave?'

'We're as mystified as you are,' said Alex, 'but we'll all know soon, won't we?'

Ella was impressed by his composure. So, it seemed, was the reporter.

'Yes, yes we will.' He turned back to face the camera.

'This is Callum Brisket in Oakport Churchyard. Now, back to Liz in the studio . . .'

The other reporters had got wind of the fact that they were there. Like dominoes, they began to turn. Now that he had clinched his exclusive, Callum Brisket became their ally.

'The lady's here to lay some flowers. Make room for her.'

He walked ahead, easing their path. Sarah followed, Alex holding her steady. Ella brought up the rear, feeling as if she was part of some strange procession.

As they came to the row of graves, Callum Brisket stepped out of the way and pushed back the reporters beside him. 'Give her some space,' he said.

Alex led Sarah to Ethan's grave and helped her to lay down the blood-red roses. Ella stood above them, her eyes transfixed by the name etched deep into the headstone. 'Ethan Sawyer'. Before her eyes, the letters began to dissolve until the words were no longer readable. It was as if they were melting. Then, letters began to return, but the words were different. Slowly, but gradually, they came into focus. 'Eduard de Savigny'.

At once, the thoughts and feelings she had been suppressing surged to the surface of her mind. She was still so confused about what had happened that night at Ethan Sawyer's photographic studio. She had watched Ethan fall to the ground, pinned down by the burning timber. There was no way he could have escaped. But, what about Eduard? She dimly remembered hearing that vampires could survive fire. If that was true and Eduard had survived, what had become of him?

'Ella . . . are you coming?'

Alex was leading Sarah away again. When she glanced back at the headstone, the words once more read 'Ethan Sawyer'. Why was her mind playing these tricks on her? More confused than ever, she followed the others.

As she crossed the churchyard, she saw the men digging down into the grave that was once supposed to be Alex's resting place. Ella was taken aback by the frenzied speculation over whose body lay inside. It was a good thing they didn't know about Eduard, Ella thought. Now *that* really would be a story for them.

'Oh, excuse me!' She felt the impact of someone running into her and then reaching out to steady her. She turned, but the figure had already rushed past her. All she could make out of him was a spiky haircut. He must be another reporter, on his way to join the rest of the pack.

She turned back again and quickened her stride to catch up with Alex and Sarah.

Alex drove them all back to the house on Shadow Street. As they opened the door, Charlie came running out.

'I saw you all on TV!'

Alex frowned and brushed past his brother.

Ella smiled at Charlie. It must be tough for him. He had been through so much. If he was treating the latest developments like a new episode of *The X-Files*, was there really any harm in that? At least he was holding it together, which was more than could be said of his aunt.

'I'd better talk to Sarah,' Alex whispered to Ella. 'Can you take Charlie out for a while?'

'Sure,' she said. 'Charlie? How do you fancy showing me your new rollerblade moves?'

'Cool!'

He rushed upstairs and moments later they were out in the street. Ella watched Charlie. He was very graceful on the blades, effortlessly twisting and turning.

'Uncle Ethan bought me these, you know.'

'I remember. You've got really good on them. Much better than Alex!'

'Alex didn't like Uncle Ethan, did he?'

Ella shrugged. 'Alex and Ethan, had some problems. It happens in most families. It's just a shame they couldn't sort them out before . . .'

'But *you* liked Uncle Ethan, didn't you?'

Charlie was skating around her in a circle. It was making her feel dizzy.

'I didn't really . . . know him . . . not well.'

'You went to meet him . . . the night he died . . . out at the boathouse.'

He was circling around her faster and faster now. The sensation took her back to the gallery . . . dancing with Ethan . . . back further to that ballroom in Prague . . . the first time they had danced together . . . surrounded by candles. She was confused. Were they the candles in the ballroom, or those in the studio? It was a blur. He was spinning her faster and faster, until the flames of the candles merged into a circle of light. And then she was dancing with him in the centre of the fire, knowing that there was no escape . . .

When she came to, she could feel the hard earth beneath her and see Alex's anxious face above.

'Are you OK?' he asked.

'I think so.'

'What happened?'

'I don't know. I can't remember.'

'Let's get you inside.'

He tried to pull her up, but her body would not move in the way that she willed it. Alex scooped his arms underneath her and lifted her from the ground. He carried her inside and up to the bedroom.

She let out a deep sigh as he released her gently on to the bed. 'I'm sorry, Alex.'

'It's probably just the stress of everything we're going through. I guess it just affects us all differently. I'll leave you to get some rest.'

He kissed her softly on the mouth. His lips felt as cool as marble against hers. She was burning up. Perhaps she had caught a fever? He was right. She should try to rest. She watched him walk towards the door. As he opened it, she felt herself already falling into sleep.

Some time later – maybe minutes, maybe more – her eyelids flickered open. Charlie was standing in the doorway in the exact same spot where Alex had been. He was watching her and smiled as their eyes met. She smiled back, but her need for sleep was so strong that her eyes shut once more and she drifted back out of consciousness.

CHAPTER III

I T WAS DARK outside when Ella woke. She felt as if she had been asleep for days. Perhaps Alex was right and it was just the stress of Ethan's death and its aftermath taking its toll on her. But it felt like more than that. What about the changing letters on the gravestone? The thought would not go away: Eduard was not dead and he was not yet finished with her.

The house was still and quiet. The clock in the hall showed half past ten. The living room was empty, but she could hear voices a little beyond. Walking towards them, she saw that the doors to the garden were open. It was unseasonably mild for November and the breeze that filled the room brought memories of summer. Everything was out of kilter.

She heard Alex's voice and then laughter. A woman's laughter. But not Sarah's. As Ella reached the doors, she saw floating candles flickering in a blue glass bowl. Above them were drinking glasses. And above them were Alex and a girl with long blonde hair. Alex looked up and smiled at Ella.

'How are you feeling?'

'Much better, thanks.'

The girl turned to face Ella. She was beautiful, with perfect blue eyes and faultless skin. Ella thought she had seen her before.

'This is Carrie, Ella. Carrie Jordan . . . Ella Ryder.'

'Of course.' Ella sat down beside Alex. One of the smaller candles hissed and fizzed before the flame was extinguished.

'It's nice to meet you,' said Carrie. 'Alex has told me a lot about you.'

'Has he?' Ella was at a loss as to what to say. She could not help but feel a pang of jealousy. How long had Carrie been here with Alex while she had been sleeping the sleep of the dead upstairs? And Carrie was so beautiful. But more than anything, it was the way Alex looked that gave her cause for concern. The lines of worry had disappeared, as if Carrie's presence had ironed them away. He looked bright and carefree – more so than she could remember seeing him. They looked so damn good together, she felt like she'd intruded on a Calvin Klein photo shoot.

'I ought to get going,' Carrie said. 'It's getting late and you guys have a lot to talk about.'

Do we? Ella was puzzled by Carrie's words.

'It was nice meeting you.' Carrie stood up with the grace of a dancer and reached out her hand to Ella's. 'You must come over to the house sometime soon.'

Alex rose. 'I'll show you out.'

Ella left them to say their goodbyes. Her eyes turned to the candles, floating in the bowl like boats in a night-time harbour. She remembered the times Alex had talked about Carrie. *It was all very innocent . . . we had fun together. But it was kids' stuff compared with the way I feel about you.* At the time, his words had convinced her. But now . . . Now that she had met Carrie Jordan, now that she had seen the way Alex acted with his former girlfriend, everything was uncertain again.

'Hey, you.' He kissed her and sat down, taking her hand in his. His eyes looked deep into hers. 'I love you, Ella. You know that, don't you?' It was as if he had read her mind. She nodded weakly and welcomed his kiss.

For a long time, she lay in his arms, until only the centre candle still burned. They said nothing, but she felt closer to him than in a long time. Finally, he broke the silence.

'I think we should move back here. Sarah's so fragile at the moment. She can't look after Charlie properly.'

It was true. It was true, but she didn't like it. The boathouse was their special, private place. There she could maintain the illusion that they didn't have these other ties.

'You haven't said anything, Ella. What do you think?'

'Yes, that's fine.'

'Good.' He stroked her arm. 'You and Charlie

seem to have hit it off.'

'I like him a lot.'

'I thought maybe you could look out for him, after school I mean, while I'm working . . .'

'Working? What are you talking about?'

'That's the other thing . . . I don't know how long we're going to be here and we could do with the extra money.'

'Well, I could get a job, waitressing or something.'

'I think you should stick around the house for now. Besides, it's all sorted. Tom Jordan's redecorating part of their house. He had some so-called professional decorators in, but they made a real mess, so he's going to pay me to sort it out.'

'You're going to decorate Carrie's house?'

'I used to do some painting and decorating during my school vacations.'

'Oh.' Was he intentionally playing dumb? As if she was questioning his painting and decorating skills.

'I'm going to go over and see Tom tomorrow. It's great, isn't it?'

'Um, yes, Alex. Great.'

The last candle sizzled and died. Alex let out a yawn. 'I'm ready for bed. How about you?'

They stood up. Ella glanced up towards the sky where the moon hung like a bright silver ball.

'I'm going to the woods,' she said.

'Shall I come? Or would you like to be alone?'

She turned to face him. 'You decide. You seem to have become rather good at making decisions of late.'

Once she was within the woods, being alone didn't trouble her so much. So what if Alex had decided to stay behind? She was used to hunting alone. Alex was still not as attuned to the hunt as she was. While she could understand that, it still unsettled her. She was also unsettled when he saw her in the act of taking blood. Eduard had always laughed at her shyness, he enjoyed an audience. But for Eduard, the taking of blood was an act of defiance against the world that had rejected him. For Ella, blood was a physical need, but nothing more.

Nevertheless, the circumstances that surrounded the taking of blood had come to appeal to Ella. She couldn't deny the frisson she felt even now as she ventured into the darkness. The woods had a beauty at night that was unknown to all but a select few. Ella was in love with its stillness and calm. It might be madness for another young woman to enter such desolate places in the daylight, let alone in the thick of night but Ella was safe. She could fight back and, should she choose, inflict the ultimate wound. Or else, she could flee with the speed of a panther, easily outstripping any mortal athlete. And even if she chose passivity, what could they do? She was dead already and therefore impervious to whatever harm lay in wait for her.

Ella's musings on her own immortality caused her thoughts to return once again to Eduard. Again, she saw the helpless gaze of Ethan Sawyer trapped beneath the burning timber. Again, she saw the gravestone that bore his name, and the shocking red of the roses Sarah had brought to lay there.

Ahead of her something moved. Her eyes darted about, but whoever – or whatever – it was, had been too quick for her. She was disorientated. It was unlikely to be a human – she could move faster than them.

For a time, she pursued the tangled paths that wove around the trees, alert with all her senses to the presence of the other creature. But there was no further sign. Within her the heat was rising. The need for blood was growing stronger. She ceased caring who, or what, was lurking in the shadows. The pain of Alex's temporary rejection of her softened and receded. Even her tortuous thoughts of Eduard dimmed. This was the familiar prelude as she gave herself over to her single, deepest need.

The whole landscape changed shape before her. Her romantic sensibility to the desolate place was gone. She was on a mission to find the one thing she needed to sustain her. No longer were the spruces bathed in silvery moonlight. She saw everything through the redness of the blood she sought.

Although the woods were a no-go area for most of the local people, there were some who had cause to enter the place at night. In her new heightened sense of awareness, she knew where to go. Travelling with an animal speed, she crossed far beyond the labyrinthian paths and made her way towards the source.

He was walking towards the edges of the wood, a gun in his hand. Whatever he had come here for, his business had been completed. Hers was just beginning.

Within seconds, she had caught him in her arms. In the temporary paralysis, the gun dropped to the ground and a bullet tore through the night air, piercing the bark of a tree. She watched this, as if in slow motion. His eyes were pointing in the same direction, but he could see nothing now – and would remember nothing later . . .

CHAPTER IV

'WAKE UP, SLEEPYHEAD!'

Alex strode into the room with a tray bearing croissants, juice and coffee. Ella looked at him in amazement. He was filled with a new sense of energy and purpose that she didn't share. It was a painful reminder of the gulf between them.

Alex talked as he set the tray on the bedside table. 'After breakfast, we'll drive over to the boathouse and pick up our stuff. Charlie's really excited that we're moving back here . . .'

'Just for the time being,' she said quietly, but firmly.

A frown line appeared on his brow, but it did not linger for long. It seemed he was determined to stay cheery. He held out the mug of coffee to her. Its heat was too much. She set it down on the tray, limiting the spill. Picking it up by the handle, she lifted the mug to her lips and began to drink.

He stood up and walked to the window, pushing back the curtains to let the sunshine flood in.

'It'll be Thanksgiving soon.'

Her stomach turned. Where was the dark excitement of their first meetings? Now it was all early breakfasts and families and festivities. Didn't he know that this was far from what she craved? Depressed, she tore a croissant apart and dipped it in her coffee.

He turned and smiled at her. 'You look great this morning. Renewed.'

He sat back down on the bed and reached for her. As his lips drew level with hers, she turned and they jutted against her jawbone. It wasn't a premeditated action, just an instinct. But he was hurt. He pulled back and stood again, awkwardly backing up towards the door.

'I'll be waiting downstairs,' he said in a tone as cold as ice.

Had they made the journey to the boathouse in absolute silence? Ella wasn't sure. But even if they *had* spoken, no real contact had been made.

They collected their belongings, quickly, without talking. They had travelled light, as usual.

While Alex fastened the bolt on the boathouse door, Ella took stock of the small timber building. Although she had protested about going to live with Sarah, she felt no sadness at leaving this place. It had all started to go wrong here. She had felt uneasy the first time he had brought her to the boathouse. It held too many memories for Alex; too many pieces of his world that she could not share.

Driving back to the house on Shadow Street,

they chatted about the weather and the colours of the trees along the roadside. They might have been two strangers, meeting for the first time, sharing a ride, but eager to set off again on their solo journeys.

As Alex swung the car into the drive, they saw that the door to the house was open. Charlie staggered out from the entrance, weighed down by a huge, black rubbish bag. Sarah followed carrying a similar load and threw it into the back of her station wagon.

'What are you doing?' Alex asked his brother as he slammed the car door shut.

'We're sorting out Ethan's things for charity,' Charlie said.

Ella followed Alex up the stairs and saw that the tiny hallway was crammed with bulging black bags.

'It's time to let go,' Sarah said, carrying another bag out to the car.

'Are you sure you're ready for this?'

Ella saw Sarah recoil at Alex's words. The tremor that passed across her face was answer enough. Within moments, her face was awash with tears and she had crumpled into Alex's arms. Her whole body broke with sobs, like waves from the ocean.

Ella reached out for Charlie, her hand resting on his shoulder. He was surprisingly calm – or gave the appearance of being so. She spoke softly in his ear.

'We'd better bring those bags back inside. I'll help you.'

A semblance of normality returned to the household as they prepared lunch and settled down to eat. Sarah had to be coaxed to join them, but they managed to draw her out into conversation. Again, Ella was impressed by Charlie. She realized that he was fuelling the conversation whenever it lapsed. It was amazing after all he had been through.

After lunch, Alex was due to go the Jordan house. Ella didn't like it, but what could she do? His mind was set.

Sarah was wrung out with emotion and decided to go back to bed. Ella looked at Charlie and saw, through his eyes, his whole world crumbling again.

'Why don't we go and see a film?' she suggested.

Instantly, his face brightened.

CHAPTER V

'SO WHAT FILM do you want to see?' Ella asked Charlie as they approached the cinema.

Charlie pointed to the poster in the foyer.

'Oh great!' Ella said, 'there's nothing I like better than watching a band of hunky soldiers eliminate a race of alien insects.'

'We can see something else if you'd rather,' Charlie said.

'No, this is *your* treat! C'mon, it'll be fun.'

'I'm sorry, the house is full,' said the woman at the ticket booth.

Charlie was disappointed and so was Ella. She had so wanted to do something nice for him to cheer him up after such a miserable morning.

'What else *do* you have tickets for?' Ella asked.

The woman tapped into her computer. 'I can get you into *The Last Summer* . . .'

'What's that about? I haven't heard anything about it.'

The woman frowned at her. 'If you want a movie review, pick up a magazine. This one's about to start. Do you want tickets or not?'

'OK, OK,' Ella said, handing over the money.

She slipped another note to Charlie. 'Why don't you get us some popcorn?'

A few moments later, they were sitting in the auditorium and tucking into the warm, salty popcorn as the credits rolled. For a moment the screen was black. Then three words appeared.

Paris, France. 1913.

'I hope you're going to like this,' Ella whispered to Charlie, reaching again into the tub of popcorn. As she drew her hand away, the words vanished and were replaced by an old cine-film of people in a restaurant. A figure on the screen caught her eyes. It looked very much like Eduard.

Instinctively, she leaned towards the screen. It *was* Eduard. Now she recognized the scene. The Restaurant Pharamond! Eduard was deep in discussion with a writer friend of his. As the camera moved shakily to the right, she smiled at the sight of the Russian ballet producer who had always made her laugh during so many of these dinners. And there she was, though no one would recognize her. She was wearing the Chanel dress that Coco had designed for her. Even now, she could feel the sensuous crêpe de Chine against her skin.

Ella was transported back to that wonderful time. That last Parisian summer before the war. A long, lazy season of picnics in the Bois de Boulogne and dancing at the Moulin Rouge. Paris had been a small town to them. They had known and been known to everyone. *Les Beaux Jumeaux*, Coco had christened them: 'The Beautiful Twins'.

The picture changed from black and white to full colour. Eduard was gone as suddenly as he had appeared. She too had vanished. In their place was a gaggle of Hollywood actors and actresses, filling the chairs at what appeared to be a perfect replica of the Pharamond. And then the star of the movie stormed into the room and all eyes turned towards him . . .

Ella felt a wave of disappointment. She yearned for another glimpse of her past.

'What's wrong?' Charlie asked.

'Nothing,' she said.

'Ssh!' The woman beside her nudged her.

Ella settled back in her seat. The story began to unfold. To others it might have been an intriguing piece about a wartime romance. For Ella, who had known the protagonists for real, it seemed hopelessly sentimental and overblown.

Later, as she and Charlie emerged from the dark cinema, Ella's eyes strained against the bright wintry sunlight.

'That was a cool movie!' said Charlie.

She was surprised.

'The duel was awesome.'

'What duel?'

'What duel?! How could you have missed it, Ella? Did you fall asleep?'

'I guess . . . I just have a lot of things on my mind.'

Charlie smiled. 'You must have, to have missed that duel. There was blood everywhere.'

As Charlie continued to extol the virtues of the film, Ella's attention drifted away again. It was no coincidence that she had ended up in that cinema watching that film. It was clear to her that Eduard was near, directing their moves as if they were chess pieces. Why wasn't he just making himself known to her? Was he angry that she had left him to die? The thought sent shivers down her spine. His anger, when lit, raged like an unquenchable fire. If he was seeking vengeance then everything that had happened so far, everything that she and Alex had been through, was only the beginning.

CHAPTER VI

'I HAVE TO TALK to Alex,' said Ella.

'Right now?'

'Yes, Charlie, right now. Do you know the way to the Jordan's house?'

'Sure. We can walk there in about ten minutes.'

At first they walked in silence. Ella wanted nothing more than to be able to talk to Alex alone. She had to confront him with her fears about Eduard. They were in this together, weren't they? If she was afraid, Alex ought to know. He would want to know.

But as supportive as Alex generally was, he became a different person when it came to Eduard. He seemed unable to overcome his jealousy. What could she do? She couldn't deny the past that she and Eduard had shared. She couldn't wish it away, even if she wanted to.

She was with Alex now and that was exactly where she wanted to be, planning their future. Eduard was a part of her past. Even if he had not perished in that fire. Even if, by whatever means, he had come back again to find her.

'We're here.'

She looked up at the house with its broad garden sweeping down to the road. She remembered the last time she had seen it. She and Alex had been driving around and they'd ended up parked in front of the house. Carrie had been throwing a party and Ella had watched her dancing, framed in the lighted window.

Afterwards, she had asked Alex about Carrie.

'Did you love her?'

'I guess I did . . . In a way . . . But it was kids' stuff compared to the way I feel about you.'

Again she saw Carrie and Alex out on the terrace the night before.

'This is Carrie, Ella. Carrie Jordan . . .'

How complicated things had become for them with Eduard and Carrie returning from the past. If only it could just be the two of them again. Like in the beginning. She smiled ruefully. Even then, it hadn't been just the two of them, had it? She thought of Teddy Stone, her ex-boyfriend. Maybe things were never simple – they just seemed that way in retrospect.

'Shall I ring the bell?' Charlie's voice cut through Ella's reverie.

'Sure.' She smiled and walked beside Charlie towards the door.

There was a short delay and then the door opened to reveal a striking woman, dressed casually, but expensively, in jeans and a stylish shirt. Mrs Jordan was the image of her daughter – the same blue eyes and strawberry blonde hair. She could almost have passed for Carrie's sister, Ella thought.

'Hello, Charlie!' Mrs Jordan exclaimed, breathlessly. 'Isn't it great that Alex is back? Carrie's so happy. Well, we all are!'

Charlie nodded, clearly embarrassed. 'This is Ella, Mrs Jordan . . . Alex's girlfriend.'

'Yes, I saw you on the news.' Mrs Jordan shook Ella's hand and smiled politely, but with little warmth.

A phone rang. Mrs Jordan dipped her hand into her pocket and retrieved a mobile.

'Hello, Beth Jordan? Oh hi, yes . . . hang on a mo.'

She turned to Charlie. 'Alex and the others are round on the back porch. Your shoes look kind of muddy. Why don't you go around the house? You know your way.'

The walk through the garden gave Ella a chance to fully appreciate the scope of the Jordans' house. It was grand by any standard and at least twice the size of Sarah and Ethan's place on Shadow Street. There was no doubting the Jordans' wealth. Ella was reminded of the mansion in St Dove's where Teddy Stone lived.

'Come on, Ella!' Charlie urged.

She followed him around the house and heard the strings of a guitar as they turned the corner.

Then she heard Alex's voice. He was singing. The words were instantly familiar to her.

> *It is something to have wept as we have wept,*
> *and something to have done as we have done;*
> *it is something to have watched when all have*
> *   slept,*
> *and seen the stars which never see the sun . . .*

It was an old hymn that Alex had set to rock music. She remembered him working on it out on the deck at the boathouse, trying out different chords on his guitar.

Now, she caught sight of him on the Jordans' porch. There was a bottle of beer at his side and he had a guitar balanced on his knee. Carrie sat close by, looking more perfect than ever. Ella hung back so that she could hear, but not be seen. Charlie came to a standstill beside her.

> *. . . it is something to be wiser than the world,*
> *and something to be older than the sky . . .*

The words touched her deep within. How could he be singing this to Carrie – sharing it with her? This was *their* song.

> *. . . blessed are our ears for they have heard:*
> *yea, blessed are our eyes for they have seen:*
> *let the thunder break on human, beast and*
> *   bird,*
> *and lightning. It is something to have been.*

What could these words mean to Carrie? Her

eyes might be bluer than cornflowers in August, but what did they know of the world? Ella turned to Charlie before Alex had even set down his guitar.

'Let's get out of here,' she said.

'Don't you even want to say hello?'

She shook her head. As they walked back, away from the house, she came to a decision. She wouldn't tell Alex about Eduard. It was too dangerous. He wasn't ready. No, she would keep silent, whatever the consequences.

CHAPTER VII

LATER THAT NIGHT, she found herself alone again in the woods. It was the only way she knew to soothe her jagged nerves. There was nothing quite like the feeling of taking blood. Ella felt at once invigorated, yet pleasantly drowsy. It seemed as if new life was pumping through her veins.

As the path opened up into a moonlit glade, she stopped dead in her tracks. There was a dark shape blocking her way. It looked very much like a woman's body.

She crouched down to get a better look. It *was* a woman. Ella flinched on seeing the clot of blood and scratches on her neck. Her arms were scratched and bleeding as well. There had been no such wounds on the woman she had earlier drunk from.

Ella's calm was shattered. Had Alex followed her to the woods? Had he preyed upon this woman? His touch was not yet sufficiently precise. Perhaps he had allowed her too much time to struggle before making the incision that would numb her.

She reached out her hand to turn the woman's neck, seeking the telltale twin incisions . . .

'I wouldn't do that if I were you.'

The boy's voice was close. Ella's heart raced. Was it Alex? She turned and saw a heavy pair of boots moving towards her. She looked up, but her eyes were dazzled by a sudden beam of light.

'Sorry! Didn't mean to shine that right in your face.'

As the flashlight moved, Ella's vision returned. It wasn't Alex, although he was perhaps the same age. He was a little taller with short, spiky hair and the kind of spectacles that people used to think were nerdy, but were now deemed cool.

He crouched down and Ella's first thought was that he was going to say hello. Instead he reached past her and directed his attention to the woman lying prone before them. He nodded and a thin smile crept across his face.

'Here, will you hold this for me?'

She found herself taking the flashlight, while he pulled a small notebook and pencil from a trouser pocket.

'No, not on me! Shine it on her! That's it, on her arm.'

Ella did as she was told. The boy began sketching the marks on the woman's arm.

'I'll take some photographs in a minute,' he said as he sketched, 'but there was a problem with my last film and I'm not taking any chances.'

Suddenly Ella's blood ran cold. Who was he?

And why was he taking photographs and making sketches of a dead woman.

She must have spoken aloud, because he turned to her and looked directly into the beam of light. 'The name's Lupus. I'm on the trail of wolves.'

Wolves! Ella flushed with relief.

'So, what's your excuse for wandering in the woods at midnight?'

Her relief drained away instantly. Lupus slipped the notebook and pencil back in his pocket and began opening a small backpack.

'I'm a vampire,' she said.

He froze and looked her in the eyes. She held his gaze for a minute or so. Then the corners of his mouth began to rise and he broke into laughter.

'A vampire! That's great!'

He had an infectious laugh and she found herself laughing too.

'A vampire! Why don't you bite me?!'

'Oh, I've already taken all the blood I need tonight.'

They both laughed again, though for different reasons. Ella congratulated herself. The truth was generally the best policy. Particularly when it was too extreme for anyone to believe it.

Lupus removed a small camera from inside his pack and began taking photographs of the woman from various angles.

'Are you a reporter?' she asked him.

'No.' He grimaced. 'Just a wolf addict.'

It was Ella's turn to laugh.

He looked hurt. 'I'm serious. I've travelled across the country to do this.'

'To do what exactly?'

He snapped shut the camera lens. 'I'm done. We really ought to call the police, don't you think? There's a diner nearby. We can call from there.'

He started off, leaving her standing behind.

'They wouldn't want us to move the body,' he said.

As the clouds moved above, the moon shone down upon them. Ella looked at Lupus. Could she trust him? What did she know about him? There was something about him . . . something familiar.

'So what do you think?' Lupus asked.

'This place is incredible,' Ella answered. 'What's it called?'

'This here, ma'am, is The Lost and Found Diner . . . best fries in the state of Maine.'

'I feel like we've been transported back to the 1950s.'

She had a sense of unreality at being here, in the middle of nowhere, in the thick of night . . . with a stranger. Who was he? She looked him over again. There was something about the set of his dark eyes that was almost wolf-like.

'You're staring at me.'

She blushed. 'I thought the police would never stop lecturing us.'

Without missing a beat, Lupus affected a perfect impersonation of the elderly policeman who had interviewed him.

'You young guns must be plain out of your minds, wand'rin' these parts at night.'

He fixed her with a strange smile. 'It's a good thing he doesn't know the truth.'

Their eyes met for an instant. There was something dangerous about him, she thought. But she was drawn to him in spite of it. Or maybe because of it. It wouldn't be the first time.

'I'm famished,' he said, suddenly. 'Wolf hunting always makes me hungry.'

'When you say wolf hunting . . .'

'No, no, no . . . I don't mean them any harm. Just the opposite. I love wolves. Always have. It's not so weird, really. I mean everyone goes crazy about dogs, don't they?'

Lupus was wired. He seemed incapable of remaining still for a moment. As he spoke, his hands were flipping through the menu and opening the paper napkin in front of him.

'But here's the thing.' His voice reached a new pitch of excitement. He glanced around to check that no one else was listening. 'I'm on to something big! You see, there haven't been wolves in this stretch of woods for over a hundred years! In the past few months there have been loads of sightings . . . from amateurs of course. You only have to surf around the Internet a bit to find them. But the government won't fund a proper investigation of the woods, so it's left to guys like me . . . amateurs, crackpots . . .'

'You're not a crackpot!'

'Easy for a vampire like you to say that.'

They exchanged a smile. Ella felt herself warming to him. Maybe he wasn't so dangerous after all.

Lupus lifted his glass and encouraged Ella to do the same. 'A toast,' he began. 'I don't know who the heck you are, or what you were doing in the woods, but something tells me we're going to get along great.'

'To us!' She drank.

'What *is* your name?'

'Ella.'

He nodded in approval. 'Like Ella Fitzgerald. I'm a jazz nut, as well as a wolf freak.'

'And your name is Lupus?'

'That's my surname. My first name is Edward.'

Ella flinched.

'What's wrong? You don't like the name Edward? Oh, I get it, an ex-boyfriend?'

'Something like that.'

'No biggie. My friends call me Ned.'

She smiled. 'It's good to meet you, Ned.'

Just then, one of her favourite songs started

playing on the jukebox. This was a crazy place – no, a magic place. It was the middle of the night and she was in the middle of nowhere. But Ella felt happier and more relaxed than she had in ages.

CHAPTER VIII

THE NEXT MORNING, as Ella slipped on her jeans, she found Ned Lupus' phone number on a crumpled scrap of paper. Smiling, she smoothed out the paper, folded it up again and slipped it back into her pocket for safe keeping.

Downstairs, the TV was on and Charlie, Sarah and Alex all had their eyes fixed on the screen.

'Post-mortem tests are continuing on the body taken from Oakport churchyard earlier this week. Officials say that the body is indeed that of a teenage boy, but no further details are available at this stage. Viewers will recall that the body was originally identified as that of Alex Culler. But Culler is alive and well as these pictures, taken in Oakport town yesterday, show . . .'

They were dumbstruck as the screen was filled with a picture of Alex and Carrie strolling through the streets, laughing together. The picture only flashed up for an instant before the newscaster turned to other news. Alex flicked off the TV.

'I never noticed the cameras,' he said.

'Evidently,' Ella said.

'We had to go into town to buy some paint and stuff.'

The more he tried to explain, the worse she felt. But Ella didn't want to have an argument, especially not in front of Charlie and Sarah. She grabbed her coat and key and stumbled blindly out of the house. Tears were filling her eyes and she had no clue where she was going. She started to run, but stopped when she was certain that Alex had not followed her. Now what?

A bus was pulling in to the stop a little ahead and she decided to take it. It was heading into town. That would do as a destination for now. Gratefully, she paid her fare and sat down relieved as the bus hurtled off away from Shadow Street.

Throughout the short ride into town, her mind raced with thoughts: of Alex and Carric; of Sarah and Charlie; of Eduard. There was no one she could talk to about Eduard and it was driving her mad keeping her fears to herself. If he wasn't dead, why didn't he just make himself known to her? If he loved her as he always protested he did, why was he making her suffer so? And Alex – what kind of game was he playing? Was he trying to make her jealous? Well, if so, he was doing an exceedingly good job of it.

What would he think if he knew about Ned? Ned! At once, her head was filled with thoughts of the strange guy she had found in the woods. Even though they had only just met, she felt there was a real connection between them. She would call him as soon as she got into town. Ella felt for the slip of paper in her jeans pocket. Taking it out she unfolded it. The mere sight of his name and number was at once reassuring and surprisingly exciting.

'I didn't expect to hear from you so soon!' Ned said. Ella could tell from the way he said it that he was pleased.

'Can you meet me in town?'

'Sure. I'll be there in fifteen minutes. Where shall I meet you?'

She thought for a moment. 'I'll be in the churchyard.'

He laughed. 'Perfect. See you in fifteen minutes.'

She was standing in front of Alex's grave when he arrived. A light rain had just begun to fall. For a moment, she felt nervous and embarrassed about calling him. But as he walked towards her with a broad smile on his face, her qualms disappeared.

'I've never had a date in a churchyard before,' he said. 'I guess you vampires do this all the time.'

She smiled at him, aware of the gulf between them. It was fine for him to joke about her being a vampire, but how would he react if he knew the truth? There was so much he didn't know about her. Could she trust him? She felt she could, but it was too soon, way too soon to tell him every crazy thought that was spinning around her head.

'Are you OK?' he asked. 'You sounded kind of upset on the phone.'

'I'm feeling better now, thanks.'

'Standing around in a churchyard in the rain will do that for you. So . . . what made you meet me here?'

'I'm trying to work something out.'

'Something about me?'

'No.' She shook her head. 'About them . . .' She nodded towards the graves.

His eyes followed her gaze and he read the inscriptions on the headstones.

'Alex Culler . . . there was something about him on the news this morning. They buried the wrong guy, didn't they?'

'Something like that.'

'Do you know him?'

She measured her words. 'He's my boyfriend.'

'Ah.'

'What does that mean?'

He bowed his head. 'It means . . . that guys like me shouldn't get their hopes up when they meet beautiful women like you in the woods at midnight.'

She smiled at him. 'I'm glad I met you, Ned. You're so . . . different.'

'I guess I'd better take that as a compliment.'

'I guess you had.'

'Not that I have anything against churchyards, but I am kind of hungry and we are getting just a little wet. What would you say to us finding somewhere for lunch?'

'Are you always this hungry?'

'You seem to have that effect on me.'

She was embarrassed. He thought she was flirting with him. Maybe she was. She hardly knew her own mind any more. What was she doing? What was she getting herself into now?

As they wove their way back through the graves, he gave her shoulder a friendly squeeze. 'You're spooked, Ella. It's cool if you don't feel you can tell me why. But I think you're going to be fine.'

'I hope so.'

'I know so.'

'You know, I figured out your name,' Ella said as the waitress placed two bowls of clam chowder on their table. 'Lupus is the Latin for wolf.'

He blinked at her through his glasses. 'I'm impressed. Not many people I run into know their Latin.'

'So, is it your real name? I mean it's kind of a coincidence, isn't it?'

'There are stranger things on heaven and earth . . . and all that baloney. I don't know. It's not like I come from a family of wolf hunters. My parents think I'm nuts.'

He dipped his spoon into the soup. 'Do you have family around here?'

She shook her head. 'Alex does. I'm from England. That's where we met.' Her mind was racing, trying to ensure that she gave only so much away.

'So you followed him across the ocean? I guess it must be pretty serious between you guys,' Ned said.

'Don't sound so gloomy,' she said. 'We can still be friends, can't we?'

'We can be whatever you want, Ella,' he replied.

She shivered for a moment. The last thing she needed was a new romantic complication. She was still involved with Alex, even if things were far from the rosy picture she was presenting to Ned. And then there were her still unresolved feelings for Eduard. No, she couldn't allow herself to get involved with Ned in any way other than friendship.

CHAPTER IX

ELLA SPENT MOST of the afternoon with Ned, returning late to the house on Shadow Street. She was met at the door by Sarah, who looked more anxious than ever.

'Where have you been? We were worried.'

'I'm sorry, Sarah, I didn't mean to add to your stress,' Ella said. 'I just needed some time away.'

'Ella!' Alex came running downstairs. He was wrapped in a towel and his hair was dripping wet. 'Are you OK?'

'Yes, I'm fine.'

Charlie stepped in from the garden. 'Hi, Ella. Did you have a good day?'

'Yes, Charlie. Thanks for asking.'

'Come and tell me all about it while we get ready,' said Alex, climbing the stairs.

'Ready for what?'

'There's a party tonight . . . at this crazy place called The Lost and Found. You'll love it.'

'Oh, Alex, I'm really not in the mood . . .'

'Ella, we have to go. It's a party for *us*. Carrie's spent all day organizing it.'

'She has? Isn't she just a regular little angel of mercy?'

'Listen, all my old friends are going to be

there. I can't wait for you to meet them. C'mon, Ella, it'll be fun. And tomorrow night, we'll go out by ourselves . . . I promise.'

It soon became clear to Ella that the party was in Alex's honour only. Perhaps it was the banner hanging across the entrance to The Lost and Found which read 'Welcome Home Alex!' that gave the game away. She wasn't surprised. Carrie might be pleased as punch that her former beau had come home, but she could hardly be thrilled about the extra baggage he'd brought along.

'Here's the guest of honour!' Carrie rushed to welcome them inside. She pulled Alex towards her and hugged him as if this was the first time she had seen him since his homecoming. By Ella's calculations it was barely two hours since they had parted.

As Carrie's slender arms unwrapped themselves from around Alex, she moved forward to hug Ella too. Ella was struck by the scent of strawberries as Carrie's long blonde hair brushed against her own.

'This is *so* sweet of you, Carrie.'

'I hope you're not angry with me, Ella,' said Carrie, just quietly enough to be out of Alex's hearing.

'Angry? Why should I be angry?'

'Well, Alex and I were together . . . for quite a long time. I don't want anyone to get the wrong idea about this.'

'I'm sure everyone realizes it's simply a selfless gesture of friendship,' said Ella sweetly.

'I tried calling you earlier to see if you wanted to help out. Sarah said she didn't know where you were.'

'No, I took off for the day.' It was obvious that Carrie expected more of an answer.

'Well, let's mingle, shall we? Who would you like to meet? How about Bryan . . . that hunky guy over there.'

Ella looked around. Bryan was indeed a hunk, but she wasn't about to fall into one of the traps Carrie had set for her.

'I'll just tag along with Alex, for now,' she said, brushing past before Carrie could stop her.

Alex was in the middle of a reunion with a couple of guys. As Ella approached, she heard snatches of their conversation.

'Man, I'm so glad to have you back.'

'Not as glad as Carrie, huh? It's so cool that you guys are back together!'

'Actually, we're . . .'

Alex caught Ella's eyes nervously. 'Actually, this is my new girlfriend. Ella, this is Danny and Sean.'

Danny – the guy who had mentioned Carrie – looked sheepish, but there was nothing sheepish about the way Sean was looking at her.

'It's great to meet you, Ella,' he said. 'Can I get you a drink?'

'Sure,' she said, 'I'll come with you to the bar.'

Clearly, Sean could hardly believe his luck. 'By the way, I love your accent. Are you Australian?'

'English.'

'English? Cool!'

As they moved away, Ella heard Danny ask Alex, 'So what's the deal with the body in your grave?'

The Lost and Found was soon filled with people. It looked like Carrie had managed to round up just about everyone under twenty-one in a ten-mile radius. Ella could tell that Alex was having a great time and she was pleased about that. His life had been short on happiness of late and, however difficult things were between them just now, she wanted him to be happy.

At the same time, she couldn't help feeling low and alone, more aware than ever of the gulf between Alex and herself. For one thing, occasions like these reminded her how very long it had been since she had been surrounded by a crowd of her own friends. Out of necessity, she could never settle in one place for too long. That was something Alex had not yet grasped. They could not stay in Oakport long without running the risk of their true selves being discovered. If that happened, the townsfolk would not be vying to buy him a drink. Far from it. She had seen it too many times. Tonight, he could drink and dance all he wanted, but soon he would have to face up to the reality of being a vampire.

If only he could see what a wonderful existence they would have if he could just break these ties. She had seen more of life than the others in this room would ever see. She had tasted greater pleasures and yes, endured deeper pains. But it was worth it. It was worth it.

'Would you like to dance?'

She found hunky Bryan at her side. No doubt, Carrie had sent him over. Ella scanned the room and saw that – big surprise – Carrie was dancing with Alex.

'Sure, Bryan.'

She could see his momentary confusion that she already knew his name, followed by a smile as he deduced this could only be a good thing. He laid a firm hand on her shoulder and guided her towards the dance floor.

The band launched into an old rock song and Ella gratefully lost herself in the music. She was vaguely aware of Bryan smugly appraising her as if she was the catch of the day. Poor fool. Poor beautiful fool, she thought. If only you knew your date was over two hundred years old, would you still be smiling?

CHAPTER X

BY MIDNIGHT THE party was still going strong. Ella wasn't having too bad a time dancing with Alex and his friends. She decided to take a breather and headed off to get a Coke. She found herself a place at the bar, realizing a moment too late that she was standing right next to Carrie Jordan.

'Well, Carrie, you certainly know how to throw a good party.'

'Thanks, Ella. I can't tell you how much that means to me.'

Neither of them seemed able to think of anything else to say to each other. There was an awkward silence as each took a sip from her drink and surveyed the room.

'Actually, Ella, I was wondering if I could ask your advice. It's about one of my girlfriends . . . You see, this girlfriend of mine broke up with her boyfriend a while back. It was over nothing at all, but circumstances kept them apart and now he has a new girl who is very smart and very beautiful . . .'

Ella thought she could see where this was going. She sipped her Coke.

'. . . but my girlfriend isn't sure that these

people are right for each other. Besides, she still has feelings for her ex . . . and it's clear that he still has feelings for her . . .'

'That's what she thinks, is it?' said Ella.

'Oh, she knows,' purred Carrie. 'You see, he's talked to her about his new girlfriend and, well . . . it isn't so much what he says as what he doesn't say. You know what I mean?'

Ella was starting to tire of Carrie's game. 'What advice would you like from me?'

'Well, I've told my girlfriend to wait . . . just a little while, you understand. But, if she thinks that this new thing is heading nowhere, I say she should just step back in and take what's rightfully hers. What do you think about that?'

Ella shrugged. 'I think your friend should make up her own mind. She doesn't need advice from me. But she should be careful. I mean who knows what kind of monster this new girlfriend might be? I'd want to be clear about that before I started crossing swords with her.'

The two girls stared at each other long and hard.

'I think I'm ready for another dance,' said Ella.

'Yes, and I think Bryan is looking for me.' Carrie slipped down from the bar stool and turned to walk away.

'Oh, Carrie. Wait! Don't forget to wish your friend good luck . . . from me.'

Ella finished her drink while Carrie headed

off. As she stepped down from the bar stool, she found a familiar face beaming at her.

'Well, if it isn't my favourite lady vampire!'

'Ned! What are you doing here?'

'I just came in for some fries before I hit the woods. I didn't realize it was "swank" night.'

'Well, you can thank my boyfriend's ex-girlfriend for that.'

'Sounds like quite a story.'

'Why don't we split an order of fries and I'll fill you in on all the gory details?'

Ella and Ned moved to one of the high-backed booths and waited for their order of fries. Although they had spent most of the day together, there seemed no danger of them running out of conversation. With his combat trousers and thick roll-neck sweater, Ned was dressed somewhat differently to the other guys at the party. Like Ella, he wasn't part of the in-crowd and had attracted a few stares. Ella couldn't have cared less.

It was only when the fries arrived that their conversation momentarily halted. As it did, Ella recognized voices from the other side of the booth. She hushed Ned so that they could overhear their neighbours' conversation.

'It's good to see Ella making her own friends here in Oakport.'

'What do you mean, Carrie?'

'Oh, didn't you see that guy she was talking to

at the bar. I don't know where they've gotten to, but he was quite good-looking . . . in a nerdy kind of way.'

Ned looked at Ella with mock hurt and mouthed the word 'nerdy'. It was all she could do to control her giggles.

'Well, like you say, it's good for her to make new friends.'

'"New friends are silver, old are gold." Isn't that what they say?'

'I think my grandmother had a piece of needlepoint to that effect.'

Ella stifled a laugh at Alex's response. Clearly, he wasn't prepared to take the conversation in the direction Carrie wanted.

'All right, Alex, so it *is* a corny old saying. But it's true. Your old friends *are* important.'

'I'll drink to that!'

'Maybe you've had enough to drink.'

'That's not a very *friendly* thing to say.'

'You know, sometimes, you can be *so* infuriating. Gorgeous but infuriating.'

Before Ella could stop him, Ned had stood up and leaned over so that his face was just above Alex's and facing Carrie's.

'So, *he's* gorgeous and *I'm* just a good-looking nerd?'

Carrie's embarrassment quickly turned to fury. 'Actually, up close, I think maybe you're a not-so-good-looking nerd.' She jumped up from the booth and marched angrily away.

'Her hostess skills are wearing thin,' Ella observed.

'You must be the new friend,' Alex said as he came to join them. He raised his glass to Ned.

'I'm Ned the Nerd. You must be Alex the Infuriating.'

'I believe the term was "gorgeous-but-infuriating". Guilty as charged!'

They shook hands, laughing.

'So did you guys meet tonight?' Alex asked.

'That's right,' Ned said. 'I'm about to head out into the woods. I'm tracking wolves.'

'The woods, eh? We've been known to go to the woods ourselves, haven't we?' Alex snuggled up close to Ella. Her heart was pounding. In this state, there was no telling what he would give away.

'Really?' Ned said.

'Oh yeah, in fact, I wouldn't mind going there right now. How about you, Ella?'

Ella pointed to the clock. 'Ned, look at the time. Shouldn't you be on your way?'

He smiled but did not respond immediately. Please take the hint, Ned, she thought. If you really are my friend, leave now. I do want to tell you about me but not here, not now.

'You're right. Time's a-wasting. Look out, wolves!' Ned stood up and eased his backpack on to his shoulder.

Alex stood up and slapped Ned on the back. 'It was great to meet you. Come and visit!'

'OK, OK!' Ned laughed. 'Night, Ella. See you soon.'

He was still chuckling to himself as he headed out of the door.

Ella stood up beside Alex. 'It's time we headed home, don't you think?'

'I want to go to the woods. I'm *hungry*.'

She couldn't let him go to the woods in this state. There was no telling what might happen. She was still trying to figure out what to do when Carrie came back over.

'Thanks for a wonderful party, Carrie,' Alex said. 'We're going to the woods.'

'The woods?' Carrie was confused.

'He doesn't know what he's saying,' Ella said.

'I know exactly what I'm saying. I want to go to the woods. If you won't come with me, I'm sure Carrie will.'

Cheap shot, thought Ella.

'The woods!' Carrie exclaimed. 'Why would I want to go to the woods at this hour? It's November in case you've forgotten and it's cold out.'

'I'll keep you warm,' Alex said.

'I'm going home now, with or without you,' Ella said. 'Goodnight, Carrie. And thanks for . . . everything.'

As she walked out of The Lost and Found, she didn't look back. She couldn't bear to see the look of victory on Carrie's face.

The chill night air was refreshing after the

heat inside. Ella had only walked a few paces when she decided to change direction. Now she thought about it, it wasn't *so* late, and she was feeling kind of hungry herself. Maybe a trip to the woods wasn't such a bad idea after all.

CHAPTER XI

A s usual, Ella felt calmed by being in the woods. She thought back over the evening and the day before. She really ought to talk to Alex about Eduard. Keeping her silence would only drive the wedge further between them. Perhaps she would catch him alone tomorrow. She vaguely remembered him saying something about them going out together. Would he remember in the morning? She doubted it, given the state he'd been in at the party.

Carrie's face had been a picture when Alex had suggested a trip to the woods. If only Miss butter-wouldn't-melt-in-her-mouth Jordan knew how much her old love had changed, she would run back to hunky Bryan as fast as her stilettos could carry her.

Ella smiled. It had been good seeing Ned again. He was so funny and so unpredictable. He was very easy to be with. Almost too easy, perhaps. He still unsettled her a little, although she couldn't pinpoint why.

Her thoughts were interrupted by a piercing scream. It seemed to shake the whole of the woods.

Instinctively, Ella moved towards its source. It was a clearing not far away. She brushed back the silvery branches of a spruce and found herself looking down at the body of Carrie Jordan.

Ella knelt down. There was blood, but nothing like as much as had emanated from the body she and Ned had discovered the previous night. The twin incisions on Carrie's neck were perfectly clear.

Ella's mind flashed with possibilities. Who could have done this? Alex? Eduard? She drew herself up to her knees and was about to stand up when she saw that she was not alone in the clearing. To her left was Alex. His lips were red and puffy and he was gazing down at Carrie in horror. Ella looked to her right. There was Ned, his notebook and pencil in hand.

For an instant, the three of them stood looking at each other, unsure of what had happened or what to say.

Then Ned approached Carrie's lifeless body and tilted her neck towards the moonlight.

'I'll tell you something for nothing,' he said. 'Whatever attacked her, it wasn't a wolf.'

CHAPTER XII

'WHAT HAVE YOU done?' Alex cried, slumping to his knees.

'You think *I* did *this*?'

'Who else?'

'Well, how about you?'

'Why would *I* do it?'

'Sorry to interrupt, but shouldn't we get her to hospital?' Ned said.

'No,' Ella said.

'Yes,' Alex said simultaneously.

'Think about it, Alex. *You* know what happened, *who* did it. Do you really want the town to know about this . . . about us?'

'I just want her to be OK.'

'She will be. But there's no need to involve a hospital in this. You can see this was a mild attack. In a couple of days she'll be fine. We just have to think of a reason for her to disappear for a while . . . and a place for her to go.'

'I don't understand . . .' Ned said.

'Think about it,' said Ella. 'Think about what I told you when we first met.' Part of her was relieved that at last he would know the whole truth.

'You mean, you really are . . .'

'The boathouse!' Alex said. 'We can take her there.'

'You're in no state to drive,' Ella said.

Alex looked frustrated, but he couldn't deny that she was right. He turned to Ned.

'Do you have a car?'

Ned didn't seem to hear him. His eyes were glued to Ella and she knew he must still be struggling to come to terms with what she had told him.

'Ned,' she said.

'Yes?'

At least she had managed to wake him out of his reverie.

'Alex asked you about your car. We need to get going.' Her eyes dropped to Carrie's lifeless body. 'We need to get her to safety.'

The neon lights of The Lost and Found were still bright as they drove quickly past, but the place was quiet. The crowds had gone home and the diner once again belonged to the loners and the sleepless and the haulage drivers passing through.

Ned seemed to pull himself together again as he followed Ella's directions to the boathouse. She admired his resilience. She was still shocked by her experience in the woods. She hadn't attacked Carrie and if Alex hadn't . . . and why would he? Well, there was no other answer. It had to have been Eduard. But where was he? Why was he still hiding from her?

When they got to the boathouse, Alex lifted Carrie inside. They settled her on the bed, propping the pillows to support her neck. In the half-light, the wounds on her neck faded and she looked for all the world as if she was deep in a dreamful sleep.

'I need a coffee,' Alex said and began rummaging around the kitchen.

Ella stepped out on to the deck, taking a deep breath of the night air. Ned followed her.

'So you really are . . .'

'Yes.' She looked down at the ripples on the lake's surface, made visible by the moonlight.

'And Alex too?'

She nodded.

'Wow!'

'Well, Ned Lupus, you may have come to the Oakport woods in search of wolves, but it looks like you found something even rarer.'

'I guess.'

'You won't tell anyone about this, will you?' She had to ask.

'Who would I tell?'

She leaned across to kiss him. As her lips brushed the fine stubble on his cheek, he smiled.

'I thought you were going to bite me for a moment there.'

'Not tonight.'

It was quiet then, save for the gentle sloshing of the lake waters and the gurgling of the boiling kettle.

'Did you attack Carrie, Ella? I mean I wouldn't blame you.'

She shook her head.

'Do you think Alex did?' Ned's voice was scarcely more than a whisper.

'No,' Ella said.

'Then who?' Ned took off his glasses and rubbed his eyes. 'You're not saying . . . You don't mean that there's another vampire in the woods.'

'It's a possibility,' Ella said, realizing that she was more certain than ever.

Ned looked at her, expectantly, but she had said as much as she wanted to for now. As if on cue, Alex appeared beside them with two mugs of steaming coffee.

'Ned, how do you take yours?' he asked.

'Actually, I think I'll get going,' Ned said. He turned to Ella. 'Call me tomorrow. We need to talk.'

Alex showed Ned out. Ella took the steaming mug of coffee in her hands, allowing the steam to spiral up over her face. The heat and the caffeine brought her back to life. She heard Ned's car start. Her own brain started to engage. She didn't have to be the victim in all this. She could fight back. She *would* fight back. Better the devil you know, they said. Well, she certainly knew Eduard.

Moments later, Alex joined her on the deck, laying a sweater over her shoulders for warmth.

'What a night!' he sighed.

'Here's what we'll do,' Ella said, relaying the plan as quickly as it came to her. 'Carrie can't just disappear by herself. Can you imagine how her parents would react? You'll have to lie low too. You can stay here with her. We'll tell them that on the spur of the moment, the two of you decided to go off some place you used to go . . .'

'Mount Kineo. Sometimes, we'd go hiking there.'

'Mount Kineo. That's good. In the morning, you call the Jordans – tell them Carrie's sorting out supplies, whatever. You'll be back in a couple of days. They'll go for that, won't they?'

Alex nodded and took a slug of coffee. Ella watched as his face turned from calm to a frown.

'I don't understand, Ella. Why are you doing this? First you attack Carrie and now you're sorting everything out.'

'I told you, Alex. I didn't attack Carrie . . .'

'But if you didn't and I didn't . . .'

'I've been trying to tell you all along. Eduard isn't dead. Ethan Sawyer was killed in that fire, but Eduard de Savigny survived. I've felt it ever since the funeral. Strange things keep happening. It's as if he's reminding me that he's still here.'

'What things?'

'We'll talk about it in the morning. I'm exhausted. We could both do with some sleep.'

'But Carrie has the bed.'

'It's a beautiful night, and as I recall, there are

enough blankets in this place to equip a small hospital.'

He laughed and stepped back inside. When he returned, he was carrying armfuls of blankets and pillows. Together they set up a makeshift bed on the deck.

As he lay down and wrapped the blankets around him, Alex turned to Ella.

'If you're so sure that Eduard survived after Ethan died, do you know who he has possessed now?'

'I have a pretty good idea,' Ella said. And that was all she would say before stealing a final glance at the star-filled sky and closing her eyes to sleep.

CHAPTER XIII

IT WAS CHARLIE who greeted Ella when she arrived back at the house on Shadow Street the next day. It was early afternoon and teeming with rain by the time she had caught up on her sleep and waited for Alex to call the Jordans.

'That must have been *some* party,' Charlie said. 'Hey, where's Alex?'

'Alex and Carrie have gone to Mount Kineo for a couple of days ... hiking,' Ella said, shaking out her umbrella. 'Is Sarah home?'

Charlie was confused. 'They went hiking? Without you?'

'I'm a fair-weather hiker,' Ella said. 'Besides, I didn't want to leave you.'

Charlie smiled and reddened.

'Are you and Alex breaking up?' he asked.

The question hit her like a bolt from the blue.

'No ... I don't know. Look, I need to make a phone call ...'

She sought sanctuary upstairs and dialled Ned's number. It rang and rang, but there was no answer. Please be there, Ned, she thought. The phone continued ringing. Damn, just when she needed him most ...

'Hello . . .'

'Ned? I was about to hang up.'

'Oh hi, Ella. Sorry. I was in the shower and I had the TV on kind of loud.'

'We were going to get together? Can you pick me up? I'm at one two seven Shadow Street . . .'

As Ned's rental car pulled up outside, Ella hurried down the stairs to meet him. They hugged briefly at the door, but Ella was aware of Charlie behind her and pulled away.

'Could I come in?' Ned asked. 'I'm getting a little wet here.'

She stepped back and closed the door behind him.

'This is Charlie, Alex's brother. Charlie, I'd like you to meet Ned Lupus. Ned's from out of town. He's been looking for wolves in the woods.'

'Lupus means wolf in Latin, doesn't it?' Charlie said, shaking Ned's hand.

'Very good, sport,' Ned said.

'What makes you think there *are* wolves in the woods?'

'Actually, there've been several sightings over the past few months. And since I've been here, I've seen at least one victim of a wolf attack.'

'Really? How did you know they had been attacked by a wolf?'

Ned was about to answer, but Ella interrupted him.

'Charlie, I'm sorry but I need to speak with Ned alone. I was going to go out, but the weather is so bad . . . and I don't want to leave you here by yourself. But would you mind?'

He shook his head and smiled pleasantly. 'It's OK. I'll go and practise my violin. I'm way behind on my homework. I'll just get some juice.'

Within moments, he was heading upstairs with a bottle of cranberry nectar.

'He's a pretty cool customer,' Ned said to Ella.

'And after everything he's been through,' she agreed.

'I was reading about it this morning,' Ned said. 'I got some old papers to look at reports about wolf sightings, and I came across this incredible story about Alex and his parents . . . the shipwreck and the disappearance and how his uncle identified the body as being Alex and now they've dug up the grave . . .'

Ned was back to his usual form, pulsing with energy. What he had learned seemed fresh fuel for the fire. His eyes were dancing with light.

'It is an amazing story,' Ella said. Then she was silent.

'You're nervous,' Ned said, 'I can feel it. You're not sure that you can trust me.'

'Ned. It isn't you . . .'

'It's OK. I understand. You don't have to tell me any more than you have already and believe me, I'll carry all of that to the grave.'

He looked so serious that she couldn't help but smile.

'What's the joke?'

'Nothing. You're quite something, Ned Lupus, that's all.' She kissed him lightly on the cheek.

Charlie was tuning his violin upstairs. Knowing that he was occupied, Ella started to relax. She needed to talk to Ned as much as he wanted to hear her. She needed to tell her story. She had been carrying the confusion alone for too long. For a time, she and Alex had told each other everything – well, almost everything. But since Ethan Sawyer's death, things had been different and difficult. She'd kept her grief for Eduard to herself and then her growing belief that he was actually alive. And then Carrie Jordan had come along and driven a deeper rift between them.

Ella sighed. 'It may look to you like Alex is caught between Carrie and me, but it's more complicated than that.' She paused. 'You see, there's someone else who plays an important part in this story. His name . . . well, for the purposes of this conversation, we'll call him Eduard . . .'

'Your ex-boyfriend,' Ned leaped in.

'That description doesn't quite do him justice.'

And then she really started to talk, taking Ned back to her first meeting with Eduard that fateful night when, as the snow fell over Prague, her life had been irrevocably changed.

Once she had started she could not stop. There were so many things that she had been holding inside her until now; things that only she and Eduard had shared. Telling Ned about that winter in Tuscany and that summer in Paris somehow brought those times back to life again, if only for an instant.

'It isn't easy to find the words to explain this to you,' she said. 'Alex found this hymn . . . he set it to new music . . .

> *'It is something to have wept as we have wept,*
> *and something to have done as we have done;*
> *it is something to have watched when all have*
>   *slept,*
> *and seen the stars which never see the sun . . .*

'That's what my life has been. And I haven't just wept. I've laughed. I've danced. I've seen more in one lifetime than a hundred other people. And I owe that to Eduard de Savigny. I can trace it all back to that kiss in the snow. That's why, in spite of everything he's done . . .'

'You love him.'

'Yes.' She nodded.

Now that she had finished speaking, she was aware of the music Charlie was playing. It was an old waltz.

'Well,' said Ned. 'That *is* quite a story. And this Eduard de Savigny sounds like quite a guy. I only hope I get a chance to meet him.'

'I have a feeling you will,' Ella said.

Ned looked at her curiously, but she did not elaborate. The violin music stopped and then, after a moment or two of silence, there was a burst of electronic music. Charlie must have tired of playing and switched on his TV.

'My mouth is parched from talking so much,' Ella said. 'I'll make us some tea.'

She stood up and was about to go to the kitchen, when the door upstairs opened and Charlie came flying down the stairs.

'Quick, switch on Channel Seven,' he cried.

Ella reached for the remote. Ned leaned forward towards the TV and Charlie stopped to catch his breath. The local news programme had just started . . .

'That's right, Jennifer, we finally have confirmation of the identity of the body exhumed from Oakport churchyard earlier this week . . .'

'Oh my . . .' Ella was glued to the screen as a photo of Ethan flashed up.

'As you know, Ethan Sawyer, who died recently, originally identified the body as that of his nephew Alex Culler. The doctors who carried out the post-mortem say that Sawyer's confusion was understandable given the state of the corpse, allied with his own sense of tragedy. However, by accessing a databank of missing persons and linking these to dental records, the officials are left in no doubt. The corpse was indeed that of a teenage boy, but his name was not Alex Culler . . . it was Ned Lupus.'

Ella took in the words with a sense of unreality.

'Thanks, Callum . . . So the mystery corpse is revealed as teenage runaway Ned Lupus. Here's a shot of Ned shortly before his disappearance.'

The screen was filled with a photograph of a smiling blond guy who bore absolutely no resemblance to the dark, spiky-haired guy sitting next to Ella. Slowly, she turned to him, her heart pounding.

'If that's Ned Lupus, who exactly are you?'

Ned held her gaze. 'Isn't it obvious, my darling? I thought you recognized me all along.'

CHAPTER XIV

NED'S FINGERS REACHED out for her chin. He drew her mouth to his and kissed her. As their lips met, she wondered if he had any idea of the maelstrom of emotions he had unleashed within her. She had waited so long to be reunited with Eduard. She had been almost certain that he was alive, and yet a voice inside had taunted her that it was just vain hope.

As he released her from his kiss, he looked deep into her eyes.

'That was very nice,' she said, 'but you're not Eduard de Savigny.'

Charlie switched off the TV and stood beside her.

Ned remained calm. 'I am who I say I am.'

'I always recognize Eduard,' Ella said, stroking Charlie's hair. 'There's a bond between us that leads me to him.'

'You were walking in the woods and you found your way to me. Now look at me and accept what I'm telling you. I am Eduard de Savigny.'

Ella smiled. Even if she hadn't already known him to be a fake, he lacked Eduard's force of character. Eduard would never protest so much. He was too arrogant for that.

'Eduard *is* here,' she said softly. 'You're right about that.'

Ned looked confused at first. Then his face turned towards Charlie. The boy was smiling up at him knowingly.

Instinctively, Ella's hand reached for Charlie's, but at the last moment she pulled it back. Their fingertips brushed.

'You?' Ned said. 'That's ridiculous.'

Charlie smiled. 'I'll tell you what's ridiculous. You pretending to be me, and a wolf-hunter . . .'

Ella nodded. Now *that* was just what Eduard would say.

'This is all getting a little too weird for me,' Ned said.

He lunged for the door, but the locks turned before Ned could escape. He looked back towards Charlie, white with fear, as the other doors and windows all shut just as suddenly and securely.

Ella was struck with fear. It was all too easy to forget how dangerous Eduard could be once angered. She still didn't know if he was angry with her. Maybe he thought that she had wanted him to die.

But, for now at least, it seemed that his only concern was Ned.

'I can't let you go,' he said, 'and run the risk of this plastered all over tomorrow's newspaper . . .'

Ned seemed as surprised as Ella by Charlie's statement.

'You think I'd contact the press?' Ned said.

'Stop playing games, *sport*. You're out of your league. I know you're a journalist.'

Ella looked at Ned, desperate for him to deny the accusation. He did not.

Charlie continued. 'You were never looking for wolves. You came to Oakport looking for a story. You came here looking for Ella.'

'You're very clever,' Ned said.

'That's immensely flattering coming from you.'

Ella watched fearfully as Charlie glared at Ned. What was he going to do? Why, in spite of his betrayal, did she feel protective of Ned? Suddenly, Charlie's expression changed.

'Didn't you have a little tape recorder in your pocket when you arrived here this afternoon? Where is it now?'

Ned felt in his pockets. His hands emerged empty.

'Oh look,' Charlie said. He held out a tape recorder and flipped the eject button. He removed the tiny cassette and pulled the tape out of the canister.

'I expect you thought that this would be the making of you,' Charlie said. 'Well, it looks like that Pulitzer Prize will be on ice for a while yet.'

Ned turned to Ella. She could barely meet his pleading eyes.

'I didn't mean to hurt you . . .' he began.

'Oh, I know,' she said, bitterly. 'It started out as a job, but somewhere along the way you fell in love with me.'

'It sounds corny, but it's true.'

'No, Ned . . . or whatever your name really is. It's just corny.'

At her words, he crumpled and fell back on to the sofa. He looked at her as if *she* was the one who had inflicted all this hurt. He was staring at her so intently that he failed to notice Charlie approach him from behind and sink his teeth neatly into his neck.

'Now what?' Ella said, as Ned sank into unconsciousness.

'Now, we have a little thinking time,' Charlie said. 'I assume that Alex and Carrie are not in fact hiking.'

'No.' Ella shook her head. 'We took her to the boathouse to recover. Alex is with her.'

'Then we'll take Lupus to the boathouse.'

'What's his real name?'

'It doesn't really matter, does it?' Charlie reached into Ned's pocket and retrieved his car keys. He passed them to Ella.

Together, they carried Ned outside. When they had positioned him on the back seat, Charlie turned to Ella.

'Now might be a good time for you to collect your things.'

She looked up at the house, feeling the hot sting of tears on her cheeks.

'Time to move on?'

He nodded. She was surprised to see that he showed no sign of victory. Far from it. His own face was clouded with emotion.

'The one thing I regret about all this,' said Charlie, 'is Sarah. She went through so much before she even met Ethan. She was so happy with him. Now she's losing everything. I wish I could find a way to make things right for her.'

Ella took heart from his words. She kissed him softly on the forehead before going back inside to collect her few belongings.

CHAPTER XV

A S THEY PULLED up at the boathouse, there were no signs of life. Of course, Alex was still lying low, Ella thought, as she switched off the ignition. Little did he realize how much things had changed since he had last seen her. Perhaps he wouldn't even know the truth about the body in his grave.

'It's me,' Ella said, knocking on the door.

He seemed in a bit of a daze, his hair all rumpled, as he opened the door to her. 'I was snoozing,' he said. 'What's Charlie doing here?' he asked, noticing his brother stepping out of the car.

As Charlie opened the back door, Ned Lupus' arm flopped out.

'Things have got a little more complicated,' Ella said.

'Ella, we said we wouldn't expose Charlie to . . . well, you know.'

'Alex, there's something you need to know before we go any further. Try to keep calm . . .'

'How could you do this?' Alex was pacing up and down the main room of the boathouse. Ned Lupus was sprawled on the sofa and Ella and Charlie both faced Alex.

'It was only ever a temporary solution,' Charlie said. 'I didn't have any option.'

'You possessed Charlie that night at the boathouse . . . during the fire?' Alex's eyes were blazing.

'I had a premonition that Ethan would die, but I knew you'd do everything you could to save Charlie.'

Alex couldn't hold back his disgust. 'You're going to do something about this. You're going to bring my brother back.'

'I will.'

'We'll find our way out of this,' Ella said, trying to restore some equilibrium.

'Will we?' Alex asked. 'Will we?'

'Oh, pull yourself together!' Charlie said, suddenly angry. 'You know, Alex, you really are the most incredible wimp . . .'

'We need some time alone,' Ella said firmly. She grabbed Alex by the hand and led him out of the boathouse.

Alex was fuming with anger at Eduard.

'How dare he?! How dare . . . When I think of what he's done to my family, to the people I care about . . .'

'Alex, I know how you feel. In many ways, he's like a child who hasn't learned the difference between right and wrong. He doesn't think before he acts. He's always been that way.'

'He's evil,' Alex said. 'He's evil and you just

don't seem to see it. He killed my parents and now he's taken Charlie . . .' There was a sob in his voice.

Ella stood still and rested her hands on Alex's shoulders. 'I agree with you that he was responsible for your parents' deaths,' she said, as calmly as she could. 'But I don't think he meant for them to die. I know how hard that is for you to accept. I know that it's easier having someone to blame . . .'

'Someone to blame? Listen to yourself, Ella. Why must you always defend him?'

'This isn't about him, Alex. It's about you. You have to move on. You have to stop blaming Eduard for everything that's happened to you. And,' she paused, 'you have to accept what you are.'

'I know what I am,' he said. Now tears started to fall from his eyes. 'I know what I am and . . . it disgusts me.'

Ella recoiled. She hadn't expected such a violent reaction.

'My life was simple before. Maybe it seemed boring to you. Two parents. A brother. Band practice after school. Vacations at the lake . . . Then *he* came along.'

'He didn't make you a vampire.' She was shaking, in spite of herself. 'I did.'

'I fell in love with you. I would have done anything to be with you,' he said as he traced the outline of her cheek.

'You died because of me,' Ella said. 'They ran you out of town because they thought you were the vampire . . . but I was the one who killed you.'

'You brought me back . . .'

'To what? You've said it yourself. This isn't what you want. I've ruined everything for you, Alex.' She felt like her heart was breaking. 'I feel like I've killed you twice.'

'No.' He tugged her towards him and they clung to each other, sheltering in each other's arms, as if from invisible rain.

'We have to leave Oakport.'

'I can't leave,' Alex said. 'What about Sarah? I don't suppose anyone's spared a thought for her in all this?'

Ella was about to tell him of Eduard's concern, but Alex wouldn't believe it.

'Let's go back to England,' she said, instead. 'We'll tell Sarah we're taking Charlie to visit his grandfather. She could do with a break from us . . . and Gabriel would like to see Charlie, don't you think? And by then, we'll have found Eduard a new body to possess . . .'

She looked brightly at him, elated by her plans. He stared dolefully back.

'It's a great plan in all but one respect, Ella. I can never go back to St Dove's, can I?'

It was true. She hadn't thought of that. Her mind raced. 'Well . . . we could disguise you.'

He shook his head. 'You go . . . take Charlie

with you. You're right. Gabriel would love to see him. I think I'll stick around here.'

'With Carrie?' Ella couldn't help herself from asking.

'Ella, I don't know what's going to happen. All I know is that I can't keep running away. This is my home. I left it once, but now that I'm back, I want to stay.'

'I don't like running away any more than you do,' Ella said. 'But it's what we have to do. You can stay and pretend that you have your old life back, but you don't. You have other needs now and society doesn't understand them. Maybe in another few years Ricki Lake will be doing shows about rights for vampires, but I wouldn't hold your breath.'

'I *can* make a life for myself here,' he insisted, but his voice was trembling.

'I tried to do that,' Ella said. 'I went back one time, but it was the worst thing I could have done. You're immortal now. Charlie will be old and grey before your face shows one wrinkle. I'm not trying to be cruel, but you need to know. I've been through this. Eduard has too. That's why you're better off with us . . .'

'Us? I'm not going anywhere with Eduard.'

'Let's talk about this.'

He shook his head. 'I may not have many choices left, but the one thing I'm not going to do is spend eternity with *him*.'

CHAPTER XVI

'**W**ILL ALL PASSENGERS for Flight VS09 to London, England proceed to Gate thirty-four.'

'That's our call, Ella,' Charlie said. 'We should go through.'

'No. There's still time.' She looked down at the ticket in her hand. There was another in her pocket for Alex. He might still change his mind.

'He won't change his mind.' Charlie's tone was gentle, but his words cut like a knife.

Ella glanced around the airport. It was busy with holidaymakers setting off on their Christmas holidays. She thought of the family reunions they might be travelling to, so far removed from the reunion that lay ahead of her. It was unthinkable returning to St Dove's without him.

'Would any remaining passengers for Flight VS09 please proceed immediately to Gate thirty-four.'

Charlie looked up at her.

'You go ahead,' she said. 'I'll give it another minute.'

'OK,' he shrugged. At least he had the grace to understand that she needed to be alone.

Desperately, her eyes roved the departure bay for Alex. Her heart beat faster as she thought she saw him approaching but as the figure drew nearer, she saw that the guy was older and thicker set.

They had said their goodbyes at the boathouse, but he had also said that he would think once more about coming with them. She'd assured him they'd find a way to make it work. He could stay in London while they went down to St Dove's . . .

'This is the final call for Flight VS09 to London.'

There were tears in her eyes as she picked up her bag and began walking towards the departure gate. Memories of the happy times she had spent with Alex pulsed in her head and her heart. They had only just started their time together. She was sick to the pit of her stomach at the thought that it was over.

But as she neared the gate, she was aware of footsteps just slightly out of sync with her own. Evidently, she wasn't the only one to be late for the flight.

'Hey!'

She knew that voice. She couldn't bear to turn around only to be disappointed again.

'Ella!'

Weak with emotion, she stopped walking and turned. Alex was right behind her. She fell into his arms. It was only as she stepped back that she saw he wasn't carrying any luggage.

'I didn't change my mind,' he said. 'I'm not coming.'

Was it possible to feel any worse than this?

'But we didn't properly say goodbye.'

She didn't want to say goodbye.

'I love you, Ella. This doesn't change that.'

'Yes it does. It changes everything. All that matters is that we're together.'

He dropped his head. When he raised it again, his eyes were awash with tears. 'I wish that were true. Maybe it will be one day. Maybe I'm just not ready.'

'Is there an Ella Ryder in the airport building? Would Ms Ella Ryder please proceed to Gate thirty-four immediately.'

How could she leave now?

'I don't think this is the end for us, Ella. I know we'll be together again.'

How could he be so sure?

He kissed her and she tasted the salt of his tears on his lips. She stole a final glance at his eyes before turning and heading through the departure gate.

'Don't forget me!' he called after her.

I'll never forget you, she thought, as she walked numbly towards the plane that would take her a world away from him.

Chapter XVII

St Dove's, Cornwall, England

I T FELT STRANGE to be standing again on the beach at St Dove's. As she watched the waves crashing before her, her thoughts turned to Alex. This was where she had first seen him. This was where they had first kissed. And this was where she had brought him back from the dead. Now, he was three thousand miles away and everything she thought they had together was gone.

'What are you thinking about?' Charlie asked.

Ella turned to the 'boy' at her side. Ever since she had known for sure that Charlie had been possessed by Eduard, she had been unsure how to behave with him. She had felt so protective towards Charlie in the aftermath of the fire. Now that she knew it had been Eduard all along, she felt foolish and angry.

And yet, as Eduard had said, what choice was left to him in the heart of the fire but to possess Charlie? If he hadn't he would certainly have perished. Ella remembered the last time she saw Ethan Sawyer and found herself shivering. However uneasy she might feel at Eduard's actions, in the end all that mattered was that he had survived. She wasn't sure what the future held for them, but they seemed more closely bound together than ever. Why keep fighting it?

'Ella, what's on your mind?' he asked again.

'You,' she said.

He smiled and reached his hand towards hers. Shaking her head, she drew her hand away.

'We need to sort this out. We have to find you a new body to possess. Charlie needs to be free. And I need to be free of . . .'

She couldn't finish the sentence. She felt the salt spray of the ocean on her face as another wave crashed down before her. There was something soothing about the motion of the water, even in its violence. The tide was about to turn and the roar of the waves helped to drown out the noise within her own head.

'Someone's coming.'

Couldn't he see how badly she needed some peace? Couldn't he allow her that? As she turned to see the figure striding towards them, she felt tears pricking her eyes. The wind was bitter.

As the figure came nearer, she could see he was wearing a wetsuit and carrying a board.

'He's not seriously going to surf in these conditions, is he?' said Charlie.

Ella smiled to herself. She knew a surfer who

would go out in far rougher seas than this. As the figure drew nearer, the guy in the wetsuit even looked a little like Teddy Stone. Her mind was forever playing tricks on her.

'Ella.'

At first, she thought it was Charlie who had spoken. She looked at him.

'Ella.'

His lips had not moved. She turned to find that the surfer was at her side. Her heart was beating wildly now as she brought her eyes level with his.

'Is it really you?' He seemed as unsure as she was.

'Hello, Teddy.'

She looked nervously into his eyes. Had he caught the tremor in her voice? Well, it was understandable that she was apprehensive. They had hardly parted on good terms.

'It is so good to see you! When did you get back?'

'A few hours ago.'

'How long are you staying?'

'I don't know yet.'

His eyes darted away from hers for an instant and she realized he was wondering about Charlie.

'This is Charlie . . . Alex's brother. Charlie, this is Teddy Stone, an old friend of mine. And the best surfer around here.'

'Hi, Charlie.' Teddy shook the boy's hand.

'Are you really going to surf in such rough

conditions?' Charlie asked. For once, Ella was glad at how well Eduard played his part.

Teddy smiled. 'That's how we surfers like it, Charlie. I might even get inside the Green Room tonight.'

'The Green Room?' Charlie asked.

Ella saw Teddy looking out at the sea. He had that familiar look of distraction that could only be answered by one thing.

'You'd better hurry,' she said, 'you don't want to miss the tide.'

But he hesitated. 'Look, could I meet you later? My car's at the top of the cliff. I could drive you home. Or maybe we could get something to eat.'

'I'd like that,' said Ella.

'OK!' Beaming broadly, he dropped his towel on the sand. 'I'll meet you at the cliff top in an hour.'

Ella shook her head. 'No. I'll be right here waiting. It's a long time since I watched you surf.'

Teddy had lost none of his grace in the water. If anything, he was better than she had remembered. He moved with the grace of a dancer, twisting his board this way and that, effortlessly adapting the slant of his body to the direction of the wave.

'I've never seen anyone surf like that.'

'I think you're still a little in love with him,' Charlie said.

There was no point in pretending otherwise. He had a way of seeing through her.

'He is beautiful . . . You're not jealous, are you?'

'On the contrary . . . it gives me an idea.'

She turned and their eyes met.

'Well, how about it? With his body and my brains, we'd be the perfect combination for you.'

Ella's head and heart were racing. At last, the tide was indeed starting to turn.

LATER THAT NIGHT...

H E THREW A fresh piece of driftwood on to the fire. As the flames leaped up hungrily to devour the new wood, he settled back into Ella's arms. She ran her fingers through his hair. In the firelight it seemed more golden than ever.

It was strange to think that the boy in her arms was at once Teddy and Eduard. Strange and yet perfectly natural. Perhaps he was right when he had said they would be the perfect combination. He moved his head a fraction and kissed her shoulder. She felt a warmth inside that did not emanate from the fire.

'I hope Charlie will be all right tonight,' she said.

'He'll be fine. And in a day or two when he's fully recovered, we'll take him to Gabriel's, like we planned. It'll do the kid good to spend some time with his grandfather.'

'What about Alex?'

'He's going to be OK too.'

'Do you really think so? Or are you just saying that to make me feel better . . . to keep him out of our lives . . .'

'Ella, I never meant to hurt Alex. Things just

got out of hand. I know he hates me, but it isn't reciprocated.'

'I can't just forget about him.'

'Did I ask you to?'

'He wanted me to forget about *you*. He couldn't accept you as a part of my life . . .'

'He's young, my darling . . . Give him another hundred years. He'll come to understand.'

'I keep thinking that I should have let him die . . . for his sake. Maybe he would have found peace . . .'

'No.' He pulled himself up and looked down at her. 'You gave Alex the greatest gift you could. Think back, my love. Think of everything we've seen and done, everywhere we've been. It hasn't always been easy, but it's never been boring, has it?'

'No,' she smiled, 'never.'

'Alex has all that ahead of him. We'll look out for him, together. I promise.'

'Do you mean it?'

He nodded. She lifted herself up and brought her lips to his. As their mouths parted, she smiled.

'Sealed with a kiss.'

He smiled back at her, his eyes brighter than the light from the fire.

'Take me home,' she said. 'It's late and you're going to want to be up early tomorrow for the surf.'

He helped her to her feet and they kissed again. Then, she took his hand and they set off along the beach towards the black cliff. The light from the fire sent their shadows dancing across the sand. And then they moved beyond the pool of light and back into the darkness they both knew so well.

READ MORE IN PUFFIN

For children of all ages, Puffin represents quality and variety – the very best in publishing today around the world.

For complete information about books available from Puffin   and Penguin – and how to order them, contact us at the appropriate address below. Please note that for copyright reasons the selection of books varies from country to country.

On the worldwide web: www.penguin.co.uk

In the United Kingdom: Please write to *Dept. EP, Penguin Books Ltd, Bath Road, Harmondsworth, West Drayton, Middlesex UB7 0DA*

In the United States: Please write to *Penguin Putnam inc., P.O. Box 12289, Dept B, Newark, New Jersey 07101-5289* or call 1-800-788-6262

In Canada: Please write to *Penguin Books Canada Ltd, 10 Alcorn Avenue, Suite 300, Toronto, Ontario M4V 3B2*

In Australia: Please write to *Penguin Books Australia Ltd, P.O. Box 257, Ringwood, Victoria 3134*

In New Zealand: Please write to *Penguin Books (NZ) Ltd, Private Bag 102902, North Shore Mail Centre, Auckland 10*

In India: Please write to *Penguin Books India Pvt Ltd, 11 Panscheel Shopping Centre, Panscheel Park, New Delhi 110 017*

In the Netherlands: Please write to *Penguin Books Netherlands bv, Postbus 3507, NL-1001 AH Amsterdam*

In Germany: Please write to *Penguin Books Deutschland GmbH, Metzlerstrasse 26, 60594 Frankfurt am Main*

In Spain: Please write to *Penguin Books S. A., Bravo Murillo 19, 1° B, 28015 Madrid*

In Italy: Please write to *Penguin Italia s.r.l., Via Felice Casati 20, I–20124 Milano*

In France: Please write to *Penguin France S. A., 17 rue Lejeune, F–31000 Toulouse*

In Japan: Please write to *Penguin Books Japan, Ishikiribashi Building, 2–5–4, Suido, Bunkyo-ku, Tokyo 112*

In South Africa: Please write to *Longman Penguin Southern Africa (Pty) Ltd, Private Bag X08, Bertsham 2013*